Everybody Loves Simply Southern

What a hoot!

"There is universality in Cappy Hall Rearick's brand of humor that has the power to connect us with the most common human conditions. Whether you live on the east or west coast or somewhere in between, Simply Southern will make you laugh. Rearick's first-hand knowledge of Southerners gives her stories the ring of authenticity that brings her wonderful characters to life full of fun and a subtle compassion.

—Poet and Author Mary Stripling, Atlanta, Georgia

Glorious, Joyful Book!

"Cappy Hall Rearick's collection of essays and short stories in Simply Southern have the distinct flavor of the low-country South, and the characters ring true, from the hilarious to the serious. Babe, the grandkids, and the fun-loving friends who populate this joyful book will bring readers many smiles, laugh-out-loud chuckles, and possibly a few misty eyes. It's a book to be savored not once, but many times."

—Beverly W. Gibbons, Reitred teacher, Hartwell, Georgia

A Great Discovery

Simply Southern is a great read. Cappy Hall Rearick's style is reminiscent of Erma Bombeck's, yet unique to the South and it's colorful characters. No subject is tabu, including "the grandchildren from hell, the spoiled rotten Cockapoo, or husband Babe." You will feel like you have had a long visit with an old friend.

—Laura Partin, Registered Nurse, Chino Hills, California

A Bodacious Book!

"Settle into your most comfortable chair with this delightful read and enjoy Simply Southern, as Cappy Hall Rearick tickles your toes and tugs on your heart with her anecdotes of the South. Immerse yourself in glorious mini-tales such as "Gloryjean the Butterbean Queen" and "By Virtue of a Vidalia." You can see, hear and nearly touch the characters she brings to life so beautifully. In our hectic world, Simply Southern is an oasis of pure pleasure. I highly recommend it!

—Author Toni Turner, Orange County, California

Cappy Hall Rearick's *Simply Southern* is Simply Delicious!

Move over "...Ya Ya," Steel Magnolias, and Fried Green Tomatoes. Simply Southern captures the Southern woman's humor and the unique quirks of the South. The characters in Simply Southern come alive allowing the reader to be swept along on their journey. Cappy Hall Rearick's sentences crackle with "smart talk." Her sense of humor and honest observations are priceless. It is a must read for anyone who enjoys sharp, witty writing. Simply Southern is so impressive that I plan to check out her columns wherever they're published. I'm looking forward to Cappy Hall Rearick's next book.

—Writer Carolyn B. Fox, Tarzana, California

It's A State Of Mind!

As a Northerner new to the South I discovered Southerners and Northerners have more to distinguish them than their accents. Cappy Hall Rearick's take on life is hilarious. It wouldn't surprise me if the nickname "Cappy" came from "Madcap." She's just that amusing.

—Constance Daley, Teacher, Creative Writing

Delicious!

Simply Southern is a deliciously funny, often touching portrait of the South and its people. I thoroughly enjoyed it.

—Holly McClure, Author and Literary Agent

Couldn't Stop Laughing

"I laughed till I cried. Then I laughed some more. This good ol' gal takes on anything and everything in the South where dog-eared expressions are as natural as eating grits. Rearick is not someone whose eggs were loosely scrambled even though she has relatives who are diagonally parked in a parallel universe. She writes about some of the butt-ugliest things in the world...things we love about the South.

"Meet unforgettable characters like Gloryjean the Butterbean Queen and come to understand that if God wanted us to run around barefooted, we would have been born barefooted.

"Not everything Rearick writes will tickle your funny bone. She can be as serious as a brain transplant. Following an accident, which nearly took her life, she wrote, "It's the top of the fifth. The bases are loaded. It's my turn at bat. My turn to hit a homer and to break records."

"With Simply Southern, Rearick has hit her homer. I can hardly wait for her next book."

—Author, Verne Freeman Hoyt, New York, NY

Readers just like YOU are talking about *Simply Christmas!*

"I reserve a prominent place in my home for displaying Cappy's yuletide delight so that my guests may be touched, as am I, by her creative work."

—Annabel Alderman, Nashville, Georgia

"Simply Christmas touches your heart with wit and joy, leaving you with an 'Aaah!' This book will be your best holiday read."

—Joyce Adams, Atlanta

"When yearning for a story that evokes wonderful feelings surrounding the holidays, Simply Christmas is the perfect choice."

—Carol Gunter, Los Angeles

"Simply Christmas is a gift from the heart. Celebrate the holidays with Cappy Hall Rearick's humor, compassion, joy and a wee bit of tear-jerking."

—Amy Munnell, Athens, Georgia

"I was hit right in the heart by Cappy Hall Rearick's Simply Christmas! I marvel at her special way of expressing thoughts, and I laugh myself silly at her humor!"

—Patricia Cordova, Banning California

SIMPLY SOUTHERN EASE

SIMPLY SOUTHERN EASE

more humor, insights and fun from
a good old southern gal

Cappy Hall Rearick

iUniverse, Inc.
New York Lincoln Shanghai

Simply Southern Ease

more humor, insights and fun from a good old southern gal

Copyright © 2006 by Cappy Hall Rearick

iUniverse books may be ordered through booksellers or by contacting:

iUniverse
2021 Pine Lake Road, Suite 100
Lincoln, NE 68512
www.iuniverse.com
1-800-Authors (1-800-288-4677)

This book is a work of fiction. Although some of the stories were inspired by the author's own experiences and early childhood memories, all characters, incidents and dialogues are, in fact, products of the author's imagination. Any resemblance to actual events or persons, either living or dead, is entirely coincidental.

ISBN-13: 978-0-595-39170-7 (pbk)
ISBN-13: 978-0-595-83558-4 (ebk)
ISBN-10: 0-595-39170-2 (pbk)
ISBN-10: 0-595-83558-9 (ebk)

Printed in the United States of America

This collection of stories is dedicated to
Amelia Albergotti Speth.

She was a former English teacher of mine who believed I could be a writer. I didn't have sense enough to listen to her at the time, but I still hear her voice today. She ignited a spark in me that has grown brighter as I have grown older. Today, my love of writing gives me more pleasure than either of us could ever have imagined. Amelia Speth was the kind of teacher who took time to encourage me because she saw something in me that I was unable to see for myself. I wish I had made it a point to thank her before it was too late.

So, here's to you, Mrs. Speth!
Thank you for the spark.

CONTENTS

▼

I'VE GOT YOU, BABE!

ZIP-A-DEE DOODAH

THE FAMILY RESERVE

THE GRANDKIDS FROM HELL

MARRIED WITH PETS

SOUTHERN FRIED, BOILED AND BAKED

WEIRD, WACKY AND BEYOND WORDS

THE FAT LADY SINGS AT LAST

ACKNOWLEDGMENTS

Many people were a great help to me in putting this collection together. I asked friends for feedback and they responded. They invariably gave me their honest opinions—not always what I *wanted* to hear, but exactly what I *needed* to hear.

Judy Hines is an excellent writer, reader, editor and friend. Her comments and encouragement helped me more than she will ever know.

Peggy Everett provided my author's picture. She is one of the finest artists and photographers on the island and one of the busiest. I am proud that such a talented woman took my cover picture.

My close friends, Janet Shirley and Marcia Dewhurst laugh in all the right places. They encourage me whenever needed and nod their heads in what I hope is a thumbs up each time I force them to listen to something I've slapped down on paper.

Morgan Howell and Rosemary Queen are both fine writers with enormous hearts. Their Southern hospitality to me was beyond wonderful. They continue to be an enormous source of encouragement and love and I'm so grateful for them.

Appreciation also goes to Dwight Plyler for always asking to be the first person to buy one of my books. How special is that?

Joan Bogdan is the sister I never had. For me, a day when I don't speak with Joan is like a day without sunshine. She literally blesses my work and me. Her laughter sends me over the top and keeps me rolling along. Joan makes the days brighter for both Babe and me, and no…it has nothing at all to do with martinis!

Speaking of Babe, the man has read each and every word of this book many times. He takes a lot of ribbing because of how I portray him in the Simply books, but the plain truth is he's a great editor and proofreader as well as a good sport. Having Babe in my life is like discovering the winning lottery ticket every day of the week!

Some of the pieces included in this collection originally appeared in slightly different form, in *Golden Isles Weekend, Elegant Island Living, The Senior Sun, Charleston, SC., or Barbara Jean's Cookbook.* Others have been published in various Literary Journals.

Thank you all for your friendship, your loyalty and your honesty. Our world would be a much better place if everybody had people in their lives like you to love and enjoy.

A SOUTHERN PRIMER

Southerneze describes the slow drawl and unique pronunciation of words idiomatic to Southern people. *Southern Ease,* on the other hand, indicates a way of life for most of us born and raised below the Mason-Dixon Line.

It has been said that in the South, life is simpler. Easier. Breezes blow softer; we are nicer and more gracious, even if we don't know when to stop talking. Well, any Southerner worth his grits and gravy knows better than to use one word when five or ten will do. We don't think like our Yankee neighbors, and we think that is a real good thing.

We eat collard and turnip greens that are swimming in ham likker, and we go swimming buck nekkid in rivers, ponds and oceans. We revere our ancestors, family reunions, camp meetings, beauty queens and football coaches. We simply can't abide new-rich people, white trash, pushy women, bullies or store-bought cooking. We Southerners have learned how to make a party out of an ordinary occasion, as long as there is food involved.

Southerners believe that honoring our people, whether living or dead, is a gratifying responsibility not to be taken lightly. Parents and grandparents are not quickly forgotten when they leave this world. They continue to touch and guide us by the examples they set; how they lived, loved and bore their sorrows. The memories they left us always live on in our hearts.

Willie Morris said a mouthful when he wrote: "In the South, perhaps more than any other region, we go back to our home in dreams and memories, hoping it remains what it was on a lazy summer's day twenty years ago."

In *Simply Southern Ease,* I offer you a healthy dose of Southern simplicity. It is my hope that as you read it, you will come away with the taste of fried chicken on your palate and the lingering fragrance of magnolias. Most importantly, I hope my words leave you with the definitive sound of friendly Southern voices singing, "Y'all come back, now. You heah?"

I'VE GOT YOU, BABE!

"Men aren't necessities. They're luxuries."—Cher

WILL YOU TAKE THIS MAN?

*"Recall the aura, the ecstasy, the perfectness of your wedding day.
Nothing could ever alter the thrill of this hallowed occasion.
Then comes reality."—Kathee Runo*

A decade has passed since Babe and I promised before God and everybody in town to love, honor and disobey. I think about this as we drive to Woodlands Resort & Inn in Summerville, South Carolina to celebrate our tenth anniversary.

According to the five-color brochure, "At Woodlands, a nostalgic breeze drifts over the forty-two private acres surrounding a 1906 mansion impeccably restored in the best English tradition."

The brochure promises that we will be "treated royally in one of the sumptuously and handsomely appointed guest rooms, each unique but with common features such as fireplaces, sitting areas, heated towel racks, whirlpool baths and personal plush robes."

I pound the dash of Babe's car with both fists. "Can't you make this jitney move any faster? This ol' body of mine hankers to be treated royally. Sumptuously. It longs to be pampered like Scarlett O'Hara before you Yankees yanked Tara out from under her hoop skirts."

Babe looks away from the road long enough to cock his head to one side and roll his eyes. "Will you quit with the drama? Simmer down and stop pounding the dash and pitching a fit. Think massage, whirlpool bath. *Personal Plush Robes.*"

I sit back and ponder the promised amenities awaiting us at the secluded, romantic inn. My mouth waters for the chilled bucket of promised French Champagne. I drool, big time, anticipating our romantic dinner tonight at the Inn's Five-Star restaurant.

Eat your heart out, Scarlett.

If things go as planned, this weekend will be a perfect way to celebrate our marriage. When I think of the wedding itself, I laugh. It was a hoot, thanks in part to Babe's former girlfriends who boycotted the ceremony.

Outrageously handsome in his new tux, Babe waited for me to cakewalk like a duck down the aisle. He looked fairly calm standing next to the rather fidgety rector. I was gazing at my groom to be, my heart flip-flopping all over the place, when suddenly my three-years-old grandson, the slated ring bearer, went ballistic.

The boy had seemed a bit jumpy earlier, but I figured a squirm here or there was normal for someone his age dressed in a monkey suit. My son, who would later walk me down the aisle, saw the child's distress and quickly stooped down to kid level.

"Son," he said quietly. "Do you remember what you're supposed to do today? It's a very important job. In just a few minutes, you'll take that pretty little white pillow with the ring on it and carry it down the aisle. Won't that be fun?"

The child's chin quivered and his eyes filled with tears. Before his daddy could give him the intended supportive hug, and before the vocalist could finish warbling a bad rendition of "The Rose," the kid let out a toenail-curling scream.

"I WANT MY MOMMEEEEEEE!"

As if on cue, the music stopped. The wedding guests' heads on both sides of the church swiveled like an out of control clock. The jiggy rector fumbled and nearly dropped the Prayer Book, but Babe saved the day.

Sprinting like Joe Montana, he reached the boy in five seconds, picked him up and quickly walked him—ring pillow and all—to his mother's waiting arms.

Did I say that the sanctuary was SRO? The guests murmured low, many even laughed out loud. Babe ignored them all and returned to the front of the church.

Bowing deeply, he grinned. "As you can see, that was *not* the bride having second thoughts as some of you may have thought." His eyes searched for and found mine and his grin turned to a wide smile. Crooking his index finger in my direction, he said, "C'mon down here, darlin.' We've got a show to put on."

He received a standing ovation.

I did *not* cakewalk down the aisle to the melodic strains of Handel's *Water Music* as planned. Instead, I hiked up my long dress and galloped to the arms of my waiting groom. Okay, so maybe it didn't turn out to be a wedding written up in *Brides Magazine*, but for me, it was the appetizer to a full meal.

By the time we pull into the circular drive at Woodland, my images of luxury are replaced with happy memories banked over the past 87,600 hours. It seems like such a short time ago that we began to laugh, cry and grow together. Since then, each day has been a gift that makes me wonder how on earth we got so lucky.

God must have been in an extra fine mood the day we met. Looking down from Heaven, she saw a displaced Southern Belle living by herself two blocks from a stubborn old Yankee who was no more a Rhett than she was a Scarlett. "Look at those two," she said to Cupid with a wink. "Didn't you tell me you needed a new challenge?"

We unlock the door to the luxurious suite that comes complete with a fireplace, whirlpool bath and personal plush robes. I sigh contentedly, bat my eyes and purr like a cat.

Scarlett O'Hara never had it so good.

TAKE A MESSAGE

"For three days after death, hair and fingernails continue to grow, but phone calls taper off." —Johnny Carson

When it comes to taking phone messages, something is inherently screwed up in Babe's psyche. A math whiz, consummate bridge player, the man has never even made a mistake when balancing the checkbook. Why this genius can't write down a simple phone number on a Post-It note is a mystery to me.

I arrive home from my high school reunion (I'm not saying which one, so don't ask), feeling beat up from having driven I-95 up close and personal with way too many 18-wheelers. Babe is waiting for me with a chilled martini and a big hug. I embrace them both with more gratitude than he will ever know.

"So, Babe, what have you been up to since I've been gone?"

Good wife that I am, I listen with feigned interest as he describes (in detail) every single golf shot he took for the entire 72 hours I was away.

"…and I did take a little divot on my first shot, just a little one. But it fouled me up for the front nine, then did the same for the back nine. I couldn't shake it the entire day. I bogeyed that hole and the next one, too. It was as though I was jinxed."

"Uh huh. Those freaking divots! They'll mess you up every time, won't they?" I don't know a divot from a diving board but I respond with an appropriate "uh-huh" as if by rote while I toss my dirty clothes in the laundry basket.

"Oh, I almost forgot to tell you," he adds. "Jack and I came in first playing bridge on Friday. At the beginning, neither one of us had enough points to bid, but things picked up after the fourth hand. We both had really good cards after that. I bid and made two baby slams…"

"Uh huh. Great. Good for you. I'm proud of both of you." Before he can autopsy every hand they played, I jump right in. "Oh, by the way, Babe. Did I get any phone calls I need to take care of before this martini kicks in?"

I look up from my near empty suitcase and what do I see but a face frozen in time. Take off fifty pounds and more than a few years and Babe could pass for Rodin's "The Thinker."

"Yeah…you did. You got one just a little while ago, in fact."

"Oh? Who from?"

"It was from one of your classmates."

"And that would be?"

"Uh…she was a woman."

"And her name would be?"

"Let me think a minute about that. Ummm…it might have started with a 'B.' Yep. I think it did."

"Think harder, Babe. I don't have any classmate friends named Barbara, Betsy, Brenda or Betty Boop."

He rubs the side of his head like our overweight dog Tallulah Blankhead does when on a flea-hunting expedition. "Wait a minute! It wasn't a 'B,' it was a 'J.' That's it! It was a 'J,' like Janet or some other 'J' kinda name."

"Janice?"

"Maybe. Ummm. Yeah, I guess it might have been Janice."

Sigh. I saw Janice earlier and we hugged, said our goodbyes and promised to keep in touch. I can't think why she would have called me at home so soon, or why she didn't call me on my cell phone.

"Babe, what did Janice want? Did she forget to tell me something important?"

"Somebody in your class is missing or not missing or dead. Something like that."

I drop the suitcase on my foot and yell a stream of unprintable words. "Who, Babe? Who died? And when? Did somebody have a wreck going home from the reunion and get killed or what?"

"Ummm. I can't remember."

"Oh, for heaven's sake, Babe. What kind of message is that to give me? Janice told you that somebody was dead, and you can't even give me a name?"

"Well now, *you* said her name was Janice, not me. Remember, I only said it *might* have been Janice. It might also have been Janet or Jeanette."

"I don't know but one Janet and she lives two blocks away. I don't know but one Jeanette and she lives in Atlanta. It *must* have been Janice who called. Think, Babe, think. Who did she say was dead? And when did he or she die, and how? It's important."

"She, Janet or Janice or whoever, said that you listed this person as address unknown and that somebody else mentioned she might have died, but that she thinks maybe she lives in Columbia. Oh…and that she's certifiable. You know, Loony Toons."

I had put together a bio booklet with the hope of bringing everyone up to date regarding addresses and phone numbers. There were a few classmates, however, who seemed to have completely vanished since we took that long, ceremonial group stroll to the tune of Pomp and Circumstance.

"Loony Toons? Babe, I thought Janice said she was dead."

"No! Janice isn't dead. It's the other one—the loony one." He starts to giggle; I start thinking I'm caught in the middle of a "Who's On First" skit with a Lou Costello look-alike.

"I fail to see the humor in any of this, Babe."

"I just remembered your friend saying that the woman in question is a few peas short of a casserole. I think that's pretty funny. Yuk. Yuk."

"The woman in question…her name would be?"

"I dunno. I think it might have started with an 'L.' I forgot."

"What is it with you and the alphabet, Babe?"

My mind races down the "L's" and stops when it gets to Lynda Faye. Not surprising since the cheese slid off her cracker way back in kindergarten.

"Babe, it wasn't Lynda Faye Gaskin, was it?"

"Yeah! That's it! Lynda Faye Gaskin."

There it was, miraculously unveiled in alphabetical order.

He's suddenly alert, seemingly happy to have been able to contribute. He even chuckles. "Janice said she was…"

"Yeah, I know. A few peas short of a casserole."

He yuks a few more times.

"Babe, is Lynda Faye dead or not?"

"Ummm. I don't think she is. Naah. Just, you know…nuts."

I take a big gulp of what is left in my martini glass, and then take my husband by the hand. I lead him through the living room and into the kitchen. Switching on the overhead light, I point to the telephone on the wall and the yellow Post-It pad just below it. I lift the large cup brimming over with pens and pencils that appear to be patiently waiting for a tender human touch.

I pick up a pen and bring it close to my husband's line of vision.

"Babe, never in my wildest dreams have I thought my mission in life was to teach you how to write down a telephone message using a pen and a Post-It note. Apparently, I was dead wrong. Now, watch closely because I'm only going to do this once."

Gator Aid

*"The reason the golf pro tells you to keep your head
down is so you can't see him laughing."—Phyllis Diller*

Babe has an on-again, off-again love affair with the bewitching game of golf. He knows he'll never be a big time golfer, but you can't blame a guy for dreaming. Three days a week he stands before his small, white, pimply seductress, which he places on a diminutive pedestal. At this point, like thousands of golf lovers before him, he mentally dials 1-800-PRAY.

"Please God, let me hit a hole in one today and I'll buy my wife a new Jaguar." Okay, okay. Maybe he doesn't get quite that desperate, but you can't blame a gal for dreaming.

Babe is more apt to promise the Golf God that he will not ask for another thing ever again. (It should be noted here that he has yet to hit a hole in one. I figure the God of Golf slaps his side and laughs out loud every time Babe tries to pitch this all too handy bargaining chip.)

Today, he jumps out of bed long before the alarm sounds. When I roll over and open my eyes, I find him sitting in a chair close to the muted TV set. He's polishing his seven iron, watching the Weather Channel and hoping for a no-rain forecast. It is the middle of April in Coastal Georgia. Talk about dreaming!

"If you want to know the weather, Babe, why don't you just look out the window?"

He turns around and rolls his eyes. "Duh. Because I'm playing golf today."

Gadzooks! Stop the presses. I roll my own sleep-encrusted eyes back at him. "Like, duh your own self. Rain is smick-smacking the deck and pelting the windows. Are you deaf?"

He turns up the volume to hear the latest update from a woman in a Brooks Brothers suit. "See there? Only an eighty percent chance of rain," he tells me confidently, as if his words alone have the power to stop the gale winds from blowing any more of our deck chairs into the middle of next week. "I gotta go. Jack's waiting for me."

Did I marry a man with a problem processing relevant information or what?

"You made coffee, didn't you," I yell to his retreating backside.

"Get your butt out of bed and find out for yourself," his receding voice answers.

Aaahhh…it gives me the warm fuzzies when the love of my life serves me coffee in bed. Talk about a dreamer!

While pouring my steaming cup of the slightly burnt elixir, I glance out the kitchen window. The wind is blowing so hard that the palm trees look like they're doing the Myrtle Beach Shag. I feel sure they will close the golf course today, which means Babe will be back home soon.

Well, time sure flies when you're working hard, so it's actually nearly three o'clock when the back door slams and voices filter up the stairs and into my office. Shoot! I'm on a roll and determined to get my last thought typed in before greeting Babe and whoever he dragged home with him. Before I can finish, however, he and his buddy Jack burst into the room giggling like a couple of teenage girls.

"What's so funny?" I turn from my computer to find two grown men dripping water all over the carpet and looking like…well I might as well say it…like something the cat dragged in. They are doubled over laughing.

"For heaven's sake, Babe. Get some towels!"

They look at each other and crack up again. Babe fetches two bath sheets from the linen closet and tosses one to Jack, who looks at me and says, "You won't believe what your husband did."

"Jack, the man left home this morning intending to play golf in a typhoon. Trust me. I'll believe anything."

They look at each other and laughed some more and it makes me envious. While I have been working at my computer all day, the two of them have been having a giggling good time. Not fair.

"Tell her what happened," Jack says to Babe.

Babe towel-dries what is left of his hair. "It's like this. I hit a ball off Number Two and it landed on the edge of the lagoon. After Jack took his shot, we went over to where my ball landed."

Jack butts in using his born and bred New Yawk accent, sounding more like the Godfather than Brando. "You shoulda been dehr! I still can't believe it!"

I look at Babe. "What happened? Did you make an eagle?"

They crack up.

"Honey, I lined up my shot and took my swing and the next thing I knew…"

Hoping the bargaining chip he made with the Golf God means a new Jag for me, I interrupt. "You made a hole in one, didn't you? Aw, Babe…"

Jack is just about laughing his shorts off. "A hole in one my ass." He puts his thumb and forefinger together. "Your old man came THIS close to being an alligator appetizer."

"What are you talking about?"

Between large gulps of out of control laughter, Jack says, "He hit his ball off the tail of a gator!"

I look at Babe. I am not smiling. "Tell me he's joking."

"I did. I hit the ball, heard a big splash, then just like he said, a nine-foot gator whipped his tail around and scared the you-know-what out of me."

"Hold on. Are you saying that you actually hit a golf ball off the tail of an alligator and lived to talk about it?"

Babe and Jack high-five each other while exchanging unprintable male jargon, then Jack leaves for home…still laughing out loud. I look at Babe and shake my head. "I have just one thing to say to you."

"What's that?"

"Nobody but a Yankee would hit a golf ball off the tail of an alligator."

Babe comes back at me with: "A great golfer once said, 'In golf as in life, it's the follow-through that makes the difference.' That little tidbit of wisdom is worth learning, Sweet Cakes."

"Well, Dumpling. My wise tidbits come directly from Forrest Gump who said, 'Stupid is as stupid does.'

Going To Heaven?
Click on Channel
Eleven

*"You should always go to other people's funerals;
otherwise they won't come to yours."*—Yogi Berra

Snow is falling in Northwestern Pennsylvania, a sure sign that spring has finally arrived. Weary as all get out, Babe and I are standing near the end of a very long line of mourners outside Jenkins Funeral Parlor. I stretch my neck in order to see around the Humvee-shaped couple inching forward in front of me, and I gasp in despair.

"Babe! This line is as long as the Bataan Death March. There must be five hundred people ahead of us."

He looks solemn and more serious than I have seen him since the Rams left Los Angeles for St. Louis. "I'm not surprised," he mutters. "Harley was loved by a lot of people."

The Humvees inch forward another smidgen.

"The point is, Babe, that those little white specks decorating the only suit you own are not the telltale signs that require Head & Shoulders Shampoo. Hellooo? It's snowing."

I stomp my feet and rub my gloveless hands together while praying that the circulation will soon crank up again inside my shivering body. My nose is so numb I'll never smell through it again. The clip-on earrings I'm wearing no longer pinch my blue-tinted lobes.

Babe's eyes roll to the left and he gives me The Look. Digging in his back pocket, he thrusts a hanky at me. "Your nose is running."

"And my teeth are chattering," I hiss as I try without success to clench them. "Why are we here, Babe? You haven't laid eyes on Harley in years."

"Time is relative," the motor mouth replies.

I move up closer to the Humvees with the hope of hooking into a beam of their body heat. Mrs. Humvee whips around and pulls her mink coat haughtily around her ample chassis. "Get away from me, you pervert!"

Harley was the sole owner of The Hawg, a biker hangout better known as Pto-maine Tavern to non-bikers. His hot wings were to die for which could very well be the reason for this funeral. A friend of ours was hospitalized after eating at The Hawg. It has never been proven that his E-Coli was the result of a Harley's Hel-luvaburger, the other specialty item featured on the pink neon marquee. Harley, bless his over-plaqued, packed aorta, gobbled down three specialties a day. He might just as well have forked over a new Mercedes every year to his cardiologist.

An hour passes before we arrive outside the door to the viewing room. While looking at my face reflected in the brass crematory urns in the display case, I pray that my frozen lips will someday open and close again. The bottom part of my face looks like first-stage Bell's palsy, and my hair? It has turned into Elmer's Glue from the snow and hair spray combination. If I didn't know better, I would swear it was wilted lettuce atop a Harley Helluvaburger.

Nobody talks so I poke Babe in the ribs. "It's too quiet in here, Babe."

He gives me another look. "It's a funeral parlor not a beauty parlor."

"Do you honestly think I'm apt to forget that obvious fact? You could hang meat in here. Well, in a manner of speaking, I suppose that's what they do."

We move forward another millimeter and by so doing are standing in the doorway to the receiving room where ol' Harley is laid out. Mr. Jenkins is in front of us counting heads. Behind him is a red velvet rope, the kind used for foot traffic control. I could think we're at an estate sale, except that nobody is likely to buy the main item on display.

Harley is lying just beyond the velvet rope in an oversized pewter casket with a red and green plaid lining. His head rests on a raggedy pillow. I figure it must have once belonged to either him or his dog. A fishing rod is propped up and anchored to the side of the casket making Harley's eternal resting place look like a canoe. His hands are folded over what appears to be some kind of a book.

"Is Harley holding a missal, Babe?"

Babe cranes his neck to see for himself, and then wrinkles his brow. "Could be, but Harley wasn't Catholic. Harley wasn't anything."

I shrug. "Maybe he got religion when he realized he was hurtling at mach speed toward Hamburger Heaven."

Babe keeps staring in what looks like a frozen frown, which comes as no surprise to me. Not with my frozen lips.

"Babe, is it common practice for Yankee men to be buried with their fishing gear?"

"My Uncle Vernon was," Babe replies, pushing me forward as Mr. Jenkins flicks his finger for us to enter the chamber. "Instead of signing Uncle Vernon's guest book, we were invited to sign his tackle box. It was so cool."

I shake my head in amazement. If I live to be a hundred, I will never understand how we lost that war.

We mosey over to Harley in his silver canoe and my gaze darts like a laser to the book in question that rests under the dead restaurateur's folded hands.

"Gawdamighty!" I quickly poke Babe in the ribs again. "He's not holding a missal, Babe. That's a…"

Babe's frown slowly widens into a grin. "That clever son of a biscuit eater," he says, obviously impressed. He giggles out loud which causes Mr. Jenkins to give him a look. Leaning close to my ear, Babe whispers, "It's not a missal, that's a remote control he's got. You think Ol' Harley plans to switch channels if he gets up to Hamburger Heaven and they don't have Hot Wings?"

"Well, if that's his plan," I whisper back, "let's hope he's taking the Eveready Bunny along with him."

LET THE GOOD TIMES ROLL!

"Makes no difference if you're young or old,
You gotta get together and let the good times roll.
Whoa! Let the good times roll!"—Ray Charles

Squeezed tightly together at a table barely big enough to accommodate a small army of ants, Babe and I are "clubbing" for the first time at Ziggy Mahoney's. We have lived on this island for over eight years, but somehow we missed out on this throwback, party down, let's hear it for the 50's, jiving night spot. I guess some of us are destined to be overdue at the trough.

If by some lucky fluke, we are able to find space on the dance floor, we intend to boogie all night long to tunes we loved, made famous by The Coasters, The Drifters, Little Richard and Fats. Whoa! Let the good times roll.

As soon as the band starts up with, "I Love Beach Music," Babe yanks me off my bar stool perch and onto the pygmy size dance floor, before I can say poodle skirt and saddle oxfords.

Languidly closing his eyes, he swings me around while twirling back on his heels like Mikhail Baryshnikov. He cracks his baby blues just in time to keep me from crashing butt first into the well-over-fifty twosome trying to remember the dance steps.

I mouth a silent apology in their direction but they are both too deep into their ballroom dance lessons to notice. I watch the man's lips silently moving, "One, two, kick. One, two, swing."

I stop giggling long enough to check out his partner. Shoot! She's counting along with him. Not only that, she's clutching a big white pocketbook as though the Hope is stashed inside. So help me, she's wearing saddle oxfords and Bobbie Sox.

"Hey, Babe, let's ease away from Fred and Ginger," I shout, hoping that my voice will carry over the high performance sound system obviously lacking reduction technology capability. With his eyes still closed and wearing a goofy expression on his face, Babe continues to boogie like nobody's watching.

Shagging over closer to him, I give him a shove, more forcefully than intended, then watch in horror as he plows into a senior dancing with a walking cane as a partner. The man wheels around, bares his teeth and snarls like a mad dog, but it doesn't faze Babe, the short-term Baryshnikov who is twisting back and forth Fats Domino style.

I love to shag and I am having a great time. I don't want to stop, but I've got no choice. If we don't put some distance between Kujo, that metal cane of his, and us then we're liable to have to take rabies shots.

"C'mon, Babe," I yell, pulling him by the arm. We weave through the entangled bodies on the dance floor and eventually make it back to our miniature table where a large frosted mug of beer awaits. Forty seconds later, that brew is history.

Wiping his mouth with the back of one hand, Babe looks at me as though trying to figure out who I am and whether or not he's about to get lucky. After a minute, he says, "Why'd you make me quit dancing? I was in the Zone. I was THERE, baby. THERE."

I roll my eyes like he often does. "I saved your life, Babe, and this is the thanks I get? That old guy with the cane was ready to pummel the daylights out of you."

"What're you talking about, girl?"

I point to the white-haired man who's now slow dancing with his cane, which I think is even dumber than a blonde joke. Babe looks at the guy for a bit, shrugs his shoulders and says, "You're nuts."

"You almost knocked him down, Babe. Didn't you see his face? Man, he was really ticked. He's probably a very, very mad Gray Panther itching for a fight."

Babe looks over at the snarler again and sizes him up. "That little twerp? Shoot, I can take him down in three seconds flat."

I look at the diminutive man, then at the 200-pound-plus Babe. "Ya think?"

Babe drains the last three drops of his Bud Lite before slamming the mug down on the table. He moves away from me so quickly that it appears he's really fixing to go after the old dude.

I grab his arm. "What're you doing?"

He stares at me like I've got kitty litter for brains. "I'm going for a beer. Want one?"

The band begins to play, *Carolina Girl,* and before I can say the words Myrtle Beach, Babe yanks me up and pulls me onto the already jamming dance floor, the beer forgotten.

Beach music rings and zings in my ears and through my bones as I dance side by side with the white purse clutcher and the white-haired old man. Through a kind of weird synchronicity, we are collectively catapulted back to the summer of 1959 when girls wore crinolines and ponytails and guys wore I.D. bracelets and no ponytails. Elvis was just a prince, not yet crowned The King. Little Richard was little and Fats Domino was not. The Drifters drifted out their songs while we shagged, and shagged and shagged.

Laissez le Bon Temp Rouler, as they say in N'awlins. Let the good times roll!

Be Still My Cluttering Heart

*"I found a letter to my sister the other day I forgot to mail. It just
needed a little updating. I crossed out: 'The baby is toilet trained,
and wrote in: 'graduating from high school this month.'—Erma Bombeck*

As I sit in front of my computer waiting for a shot of inspiration, I dare to glance around me. This room is so cluttered it resembles a crammed refrigerator. I keep wondering if any of it is alive. I could swear it's growing.

I count Post-it notes stuck here and there but lose count at 266. I'm pretty sure most were "posted" to remind me of a party long since passed or somebody's birthday.

If I try real hard I can successfully avert my eyes from the two nasty looking cups of cold coffee or the pile of unopened snail mail scattered around the room.

Taking a not-so-quick inventory, I round up eleven pairs of cheap reading glasses, a container of waxed dental floss way too knotted up to be of any use, four long-standing unpaid bills, hundreds of pencils and pens, a can of air freshener used to counteract the after effects of my Chinese lunches and a Partridge in a Pear Tree. There are boxes all over the room and they're staring at me with an attitude. Any day now, I expect the CDC, decked out in bio-chemical suits with matching headgear, to storm the place.

I pick up a diffused asthma inhaler that has taken up residence under a pile of printouts that I should pitch. I hold it up to the light and wonder who it might belong to and if they managed to survive their last attack. I don't have asthma. Neither does Babe.

The cleaning lady comes every two weeks. I hear her outside my closed office door as she slows down to listen for sounds of life. An inquisitive woman, she probably wonders what illegal or illicit things I'm up to in this room to which she has been forbidden entry. It's not illegal to be a sloppy office keeper, and I can guarantee it is not illicit.

The truth of the matter is, I love my mess, my clutter, my thousands of Post-it notes. Other areas of the house can usually pass the white glove test. I'm a pretty good picker-upper. Not by Martha Stewart standards maybe, and not by the standards set by my friend Bev, well known for color coordinating cold cuts in her refrigerator. I choose to save up the slapdash, slovenly side of myself so I can dump it all in my own space. I'm okay with that as long as I can keep the CDC from breaking down the door.

Babe's ex-wife, Harriet Homemaker, is the antithesis of me. Give her two days and she could make Martha Stewart's empire drop out of sight. Harriet cooks supper before breakfast is over, bakes bread every day and vacuum cleans her carpet long before the warranty is up.

Her shelves are not lined with everyday shelf paper, but with cloth that matches her everyday china. Once a week she takes everything out of the cabinets so she can wash, starch and iron the cloth liners. Does the phrase *somebody needs to get a life* come to your mind as quickly as it does to mine?

Occasionally I ask Babe if he would love me more if I were like Harriet Homemaker. "Like for instance, if I baked occasionally instead of buying the frozen stuff."

He wrinkles his brow and takes far too long to answer, but I don't let that bother me. Often Babe does things like that so I will think he is being clever.

"Are you talking homemade rhubarb pie from scratch, with you rolling out the dough instead of using a ready-made pie crust?"

I roll my eyes. "Rhubarb? Get real, Babe."

"Okay, okay. How about baking bread using my mother's recipe? That's what you meant, right?"

If I don't quit rolling up my eyes, they're liable to get stuck. "Bread, schemed." I grab a loaf of store-bought and dangle it in front of his face. "If it was good enough for Lil' Miss Sunbeam, it's good enough for us."

Babe's brows begin to make pleats on his forehead. Clearly, his tush is in a crack. He knows it; I know it. He must come up with THE right answer, preferably similar to the response he gives me when I ask him, "Babe, do these jeans make my butt look too big?"

He clears his throat. "Honey, as long as you don't force hog jowls or chitterlings down my throat, and as long as you don't expect me to wade through all that stuff you've got growing in your office, I promise never to trade you in for my ex."

That Babe! It might take him a minute or two to think up the right words, but when he does? Why, he's the same silver tongue devil I fell in love with.

I OINK FOR BARBECUE

"Anyone with a lick of sense knows that you can't make
good barbeque and comply with the health code."—John Edgerton

"When was the first time you ate barbecue," Yankee husband Babe asks.

We are on our way to Sonny's BBQ Restaurant where Babe will try to consume enough food to feed a small continent.

"Are you kidding? I was weaned on barbecue. Dukes' Barbeque, a South Carolina icon."

A plate of the Duke's delicacy consisted of greasy pork cooked on a spit all night, and pretty much all the following day. This fine-tuned method of culinary expertise took place in back of a small building made out of concrete blocks.

"I remember that place. You took me there once," Babe says as though recalling what I would consider a peak experience.

"Right. You insisted on unsweetened ice tea and everybody in there stared at you. That's how they knew you were a Yankee."

Inside the hut, back in the kitchen, a lot of fat people cooked up pork hash to pile on top of steamed white rice. Another pair of large hands stayed busy cutting up green cabbage and onions to make the most delicious coleslaw in the world.

Babe interrupts my musing. "Oil Cloth on the tables. I couldn't get over that. I hadn't seen oil cloth since 1944."

"Au contraire!" I have to laugh.

"Do you remember that loaf of white bread on every table?" He's on a roll. "You could squeeze it into any shape you wanted to."

Moving to Georgia has brought me new barbecue taste sensations. Unlike our Carolina neighbors, Georgians see fit to create a red sauce for pork and serve it with a bowl of Brunswick Stew. That's okay, but for my Carolina taste buds, nothing comes close to good ol' Dukes pork barbecue and a plate of hash and rice.

When I was growing up (and being weaned), meat, hash over rice, and cole-slaw was the standard plate offered at Dukes. Now, in addition to the pork, there is a buffet that includes fried, barbecued and baked chicken, collard greens, potatoes (for the Yankees) and greasy string beans. Cornbread, of course and 'nana pudding for which nobody ever leaves enough room. What can I say? For a Southerner, it's a genuine died and gone to heaven food frenzy.

Once I asked my son Madison (a barbecue connoisseur because he was also weaned on Dukes) if he had ever learned the recipe for that delicious hash.

He looked at me like I had pork bellies for brains and said, "Mama, you don't wanna know."

I think maybe he was right.

Not too long ago, some graduates from my high school set up a web site and for over a month, we chatted up barbecue to beat the band. The good, bad and you wouldn't eat that Q if you were on death row close to midnight and looking at your last meal! I told Babe about it.

"Somebody from my old high school suggested a barbecue contest to see how far our South Carolina food tastes might have traveled over the years."

Babe throws me a knowing smirk. "I don't need a crystal ball to figure out the results of that contest."

"You're right, Babe. As a whole, Georgia was pretty low on the One to Ten Q Scoreboard, except for Sonny's because he has restaurants in states even north of the Mason Dixon Line."

"How dare he?"

Babe is starting to get on my last nerve with his unsouthern comments. It's only a matter of time before he starts carrying on about the use of the word "y'all." After all these years and my many explanations, he still doesn't get it.

"As you predicted with your know-it-all attitude, Babe, South Carolina was the Super Bowl Champion of Barbecued Pork. Eastern North Carolina, you might like to know, was a close runner-up."

"Now you're talking my language, the one my tummy understands," says Babe. "I cast my vote for North Carolina Barbecue. How could an old Wolf-packer do otherwise?"

"You're just saying that because you love vinegar, Babe. I swannee! You'd eat vinegar on pecan pie if I'd let you."

Babe throws me a look. "Not necessarily."

"Well, I especially like the way they cook collard greens in pork drippings up in North Carolina! Yum!" (In the words of my son Madison, you really didn't want to know that, did you?)

"I figure it's like this, Babe. For real good barbecue, the kind you DARE NOT tell your cardiologist about, there's no place to go but up North."

Babe makes a big show of cleaning out his ears. "Whoa! Did I hear you right? Up north as in Yankee Land?"

"Silly boy. I'm talking about up north from Georgia to the Carolinas. Any other barbecue will just leave a bad taste in your mouth."

A Few Tricks Short of a Full Deck

"Bridge is essentially a social game, but unfortunately it attracts a substantial number of antisocial people."—Alan Truscot

God only knows why I agreed to go on a bridge cruise. For the first time in my entire life, I am seated at a duplicate bridge table with Babe and two complete strangers, neither of whom has made a sound to indicate that they are still breathing. They didn't even blink when I stuck M&M's up my nose and chirped, "Bet you can't do this!" I'm pretty sure they are comatose.

I gaze toward the porthole window located behind Babe's head and try to remember the feel of warm Caribbean sun. I imagine myself on deck while a salty spray of seawater makes my hair and eyelashes droop like week-old celery stalks. In my mind's eye, my pink cotton shorts show off my tanned, plumper than I care to discuss, legs. No pedicure, but other than the mind's eye in my own head, who's looking?

I am jerked back to reality. "Ahem. It's your bid."

Like a game of Fifty-Two Pickup, my reverie is shattered by the sudden intrusion of the corpse to my left, the one I had wrongfully assumed to be knee-deep in a coma. I bite my tongue to keep from welcoming him back from the nether world.

Beseechingly, I stare at Babe across from me. My eyes scream the message: *What do I do now? Give me a freaking hint!*

He's wearing a scary smile which makes me suspect a comatose epidemic, but he blinks a couple of times. It's the only thing stopping me from checking his pulse. His smile disappears and he mouths the word, "BID."

I study my cards with more diligence than I did for my SAT's, counting and re-counting the face card points, adding in doubletons and singletons. Not a great hand, but I'm able to scrape together fourteen stingy points, which means that I'm obligated to bid. I would pass, but I fear the comatose god might freak out and make me one of *them*.

"One club," I whimper in a voice so small that even I don't recognize it. (A one-club bid is a bridge slight-of-hand designed to fool the opponents into thinking that the bidder is very aware of Gerber not being just for babies anymore.) Or is that Stayman? Uh oh.

Babe's eyes roll around in his head more than they usually do. He points to something at the edge of the table to my right, and when I take a look, the corpse to my right is pointing to it as well.

"What?" I ask, looking first to Babe and then to the cadaver.

The corpse leans much too close to my comfort zone and in a very loud voice says, "YOU HAVE TO USE THE BOX!"

I think maybe the virus has gone to her brain. I should just humor her.

"The box?" I ask in a sugary-sweet voice that has no resemblance to mine at all. "What box?"

She shakes her head, points and snorts. "*THAT* BOX," she yells nearly scaring me into a grand slam. "THE BIDDING BOX!" Following her gaze, I notice for the first time that there is a small box attached to the side of the table. Aha! Now I get it.

Smiling like a flight attendant, I lean down very close to my box. Clearing my throat, I shout into it, "ONE CLUB!"

The bid is barely out of my mouth when the ship lurches violently to the side. I shriek. "OH MY GAWD! WE'RE GOING DOWN!"

Babe stops laughing long enough to pointedly blink his eyes. In a voice much too calm, he says, "No, darling. We are not going *down* unless you screw *up*. Just play your hand and everything will be just fine."

Clearly embarrassed, he stops blinking and does his now-famous eye roll, directing it at both of the cadavers. I'm pretty sure he regrets not coughing up fifty bucks earlier today when I said I needed to make a donation to the hungry slot machines. Hey, charity begins at home.

"Babe, in case you are racing toward unconsciousness and didn't notice, the freaking boat is doing a boogie-woogie. Where are the freaking life jackets?" With my teeth firmly clenched, my eyes frantically search the room for floatation devices.

Our soundless opponents did not react at all to the lurch, lending weight to my conviction that they are in Nether-Netherland. With cards held close to their faces, they look like mannequins. Silently, the stiff to my left slaps a "PASS" card down on the table in front of him.

Now I get it. He's not dead. He's not even in a coma. The poor man is a deaf mute. Is my face red or what?

In seconds, Babe slams a big red card down on the table that reads, STOP!

He is really scaring me now. I don't know what I've done wrong so how can I stop? Before I can ask, however, he smacks down a "FIVE CLUBS" card while glaring at me and mouthing the same words. Duh! *I'm* not the deaf mute here.

Slowly, the East corpse draws a "DOUBLE" card from her little black box then drops it on the table while I wiggle.and waggle and wonder why nobody else in the room is thinking TITANTIC. I am too confused to notice that nobody but me has spoken into his or her little box, and way too intimidated by my partner's last bid to do much more than breathe in shallow gasps. Babe took us to game after I bid that measly one-club, and that dead woman doubled us. Oh, lord have mercy.

The coma epidemic must have something to do with those boxes as well as the cards they keep slapping down on the table. But what? They are all staring at me as if waiting for something, but I am not about to look directly into their eyes. I don't want what they've got.

"It's your bid," Babe says to me. Apparently, he has not yet come down with a full-blown case. Where there's life there's hope. Thank you, Jesus.

Babe clears his throat again as if to underscore his previous sentence.

"My bid?" The ship rolls, the room spins and my head follows along. I may throw up.

Babe feigns a cough while I glare at him for directives. He does a darting thing with his eyes, which I figure is a signal for me to pass. Like I'd consider doing anything else when I'm holding a whopping three clubs in my hand, he just raised my one-club bid to FIVE, and we are doubled?

"PASS!" I say out loud, which brings the director racing over to our table.

"What's the problem here?" He has a shushy voice and he's wearing coke-bottle glasses and a pencil-thin mustache. If I didn't know better, I'd swear he is the magician who was the shipboard entertainment last night.

Babe's face turns as red as his STOP card. "No problem at all, Lance." My husband is practically mewing. "We've got ourselves a beginner, that's all."

Lance gawks at me as though I am the germ responsible for spreading the coma epidemic. He tosses his head and sniffs before prissing away without saying another word. I think he enjoys shushing people.

West, north and east all stare holes in me while waiting for my next move. I look from one to the other and my face begins to glisten with perspiration. Nobody else seems to notice that two people at my table are nearly done for. It seems that nobody else is the least bit concerned that this freaky virus could spread like Parkway all over the ship by dinnertime, if the ship doesn't sink first.

I close my eyes and think yoga. "Uuummmmm."

I don't dare *uuummmm* out loud or Lance might prance himself over here again.

"Uuummmmm." I am on a cruise ship in the dead of winter. There are no other ships in sight but there is something in the water. I can see it!

"Uuummmmm. It is white, it is huge and it does *not* look like Moby Dick."

If I keep on uuummmmming, and if I truly believe, there's a good chance I can manifest an iceberg before I have to play out this freaking five-club bid.

"Uuummmmm. Jesus hold my hand."

The MRB Band-Aids

*"Q: How many men does it take to find a quart
of milk in the refrigerator?
A: Nobody knows because it hasn't happened yet."*

I am on fire with a new mission and I'm asking for the support of other women who have lived with a man legally or illegally. Their input will be an invaluable aid in my quest to find a cure for the *previously* unidentified condition now known as MRB, or Male Refrigerator Blindness.

Women everywhere know what I'm talking about. But what they may not know is that Refrigerator Blindness is genetic; it is passed down from father to son, like body hair and permanent immaturity. Little boy babies pop right out of the womb with the MRB Syndrome, but it doesn't rear its ugly head until he is approximately two feet tall.

At first, the symptoms may not be recognizable because they are dormant until the very moment he pulls open the refrigerator door for the first time. At this point, the condition is automatically activated. I am sorry to report that all research data on the subject leads me to believe that there is no known cure at this time.

It happens like this: Suddenly, those bright baby blues you fell in love with oh so many years ago, turn to dull, lifeless orbs from which the male sees absolutely nothing inside the fridge. His lips part slightly and there is a noticeable trickle of drool making its way south as his stupor becomes more pronounced. After no less than five minutes, while staring, sock-footed at the white carton with M-I-L-K printed in bright red letters, he will call out for assistance. Loudly.

"Honey, where's the milk?"

Some men have been known to stand in front of a refrigerator with the door open until the bulb blows leaving him in complete darkness. Others may stand there until the lettuce wilts.

Those men have a full-blown case of Refrigerator Blindness and they need help.

Women of the world, there is promising news on the horizon. Even though there is no known cure, I have devised *two* possible "band-aids" for the problem. I was driven to do this because Babe's disease is so far advanced that it scares me silly.

In the first experiment, I glue heavy-duty Velcro on the underside of a tape recorder and then stick another piece to the inside of the refrigerator. As soon as Babe opens the fridge door, a pre-recorded tape of my voice automatically plays the following:

"Look directly in front of you, Babe. Do not blink. Place your right hand straight out, parallel to your nose, then lower it eight inches. You are now touching the top of that thing known to everyone in the civilized world as a carton of milk.

"Grasp the carton firmly with your hand, then take two steps back. This will allow the refrigerator door to close all by itself before everything inside dies a slow death.

"Your normal vision should slowly return at this time. Turn left and walk over to the first upper cabinet you see, pull it open and remove a clear cylinder that most normal people pour liquids into that they intend to drink. It is called a glass. Pour the milk from the carton into the glass, put the glass up to your lips and sip.

"If you have a problem with these directions, do *not* call me. Call Dr. Phil."

The second experiment is somewhat easier. I glue pictures of big boobs onto the surface of anything Babe might possibly think of removing from the fridge.

I considered drawing a detailed map to designate the exact spot where the milk or other items are located. I gave up on that idea, however, when I realized that Refrigerator Blindness can only be cured by direct intervention administered by a wife, significant live-in OR anatomically correct pictures of big boobies preferably in living color. Besides, asking Babe to look at a map is too much like asking for directions. My man doesn't do either one.

For me, time is a commodity and since I'm inching closer and closer to bankruptcy, I hope to enlist a few good women to help me spread the MRB word. I realize I'll never win the Nobel Prize for finding a cure, but perhaps someday I'll receive a plaque shaped like a refrigerator, an award from grateful women all over the world for sharing my Band-Aids and helping their men to survive Male Refrigerator Blindness.

Check it out at: <u>www.mrbandaids.com</u>

CHRISTMAS COMES BUT ONCE A YEAR

*"I stopped believing in Santa Claus when
my mother took me to see him in a department store,
and he asked for my autograph."*—Shirley Temple

Babe was determined to buy a pre-lighted artificial tree this year, much to my chagrin. "What's up with you and live trees," he asked me. "Just buy some of that Christmas scent in the spray can. It's the same thing and it doesn't leave needles all over the house."

"It smells like Lysol," I told him, "and it can never replace the fragrance of fresh greenery."

I should say at this point that Babe does not have the will power to turn down a bargain. He is driven. The man can smell a good deal fifty miles away. Therefore, like a bird dog going after his prey, he spent hour after hour on his computer, comparing prices, sizes and ultimately even the cost of shipping.

I decided early on to stay out of his way, so what better place than in the kitchen? I was cooking supper when I heard him shout, "Great Jumping Jingle Jangle! I've found the perfect tree!"

It was at Costco and the price was better than any other in his quest. There was, however, a catch. We would need to drive down to Jacksonville on Thanksgiving Saturday, and everybody knows that no sane person goes anywhere near a discount store the weekend following Turkey Day. Operative word? SANE.

Gridlock on the island causeway with a Category 5 hurricane closing in fast would have caused less of a hassle.

"Maybe we should just buy a tree like we've done every other year," I suggested.

Babe turned up his nose at that. "Nope. They don't grow them big enough."

His thinking was that since the ceiling in our great room is 18 feet tall and vaulted, we should buy an extra tall tree. "Last year," he reminded me, "that live six-footer looked underdeveloped, like it was stunted."

He was right about that. In fact, it looked so out of place and forlorn that we left it up until after Valentine's Day so it wouldn't go to the tree shredder with an inferiority complex.

We arrived at Costco and as soon as we got inside, Babe spied the object of his weeklong search. "There it is," he said breathlessly. "There's our tree. Is it incredible or what?"

I looked up and up and up. "It's kinda tall, isn't it? How will we ever get an angel on top?"

He stared at me as though I had been sampling the bourbon-laced eggnog again. "While it is true that it's tall, it will fit nicely with our high ceiling. Besides, we're saving eighty bucks on shipping."

I turbo sigh. "Whatever. Just buy the thing and let's get out of here." I glanced behind him. "Babe, do you remember when we were in the parking lot and you snuck into that space you thought was vacant?" He nods his head, obviously more interested in gazing at Paul Bunyan's answer to Fa-la-la than in anything I might say.

"Well," I whisper, "the woman who was waiting on that space you stole is standing right behind you, and if looks could kill…"

When he spun around, he came eyeball to eyeball with a woman shaped like a Humvee and carrying a pocketbook the size of a BarkaLounger. Had she pulled out an AK-47 and started shooting up the place, I'd have been the only one in the store who saw it coming.

Babe turned back to me and whispered, "I'll pay for the tree. You drive the getaway car, okay?"

Five slow hours later we arrived back home with our new Christmas tree. It was packaged in two separate boxes, each one equal to the size and weight of a Volkswagen. We got them upstairs, unloaded and assembled into one 12-foot tall tree complete with 2,500 pre-strung lights. I'm telling you, it was a fait accompli.

In my wildest imagining, I never dreamed our great room would ever look like Rockefeller Center. It is so bright in there that we risk permanent corneal damage if we pass through without sunshades. The dog can't stop nosing around in search of a trunk on which to hike up his leg. Any time now, I expect the Rockettes, dressed in skimpy Santa outfits, to appear in a chorus line hiking up their legs.

We'll need to call 911 to get that tree unassembled and back in the boxes. In fact, this tree may well follow in the footsteps of its predecessor by hanging around until way after the holidays…like maybe until Babe and I leave here to begin celebrating our final Christmas days in a nearby convalescent home!

THE MUSIC NEVER ENDS

"How do you keep the music playing? How do you make it last?
How do you keep the song from fading too fast?"—Alan and Marilyn Bergman

"Snails? You're cooking *snails* for our anniversary dinner?" Babe's face was a frozen mask of horror. "I don't like snails. I like fast food."

I closed my eyes and silently counted to ten. "Very funny. We're not eating snails for dinner. We're having escargot for the first course. And, in case you haven't noticed, you and I are not exactly normal. Don't you think our taste in food should reflect that?"

He rolled his eyes. "What are you cooking up for dessert? Grasshopper Pie?"

For weeks I had been wishing we could spend more time alone. Finally, I came up with the idea of preparing a romantic anniversary dinner at home. My plan however, was flying south faster than a Canadian goose the day before Christmas.

"Tonight, Babe," I persisted, "let's sit across a candlelit table from each other and remember the fun times we've had over the years. I'll laugh at your bad jokes and you can say, 'Yummy' to my less than perfect cooking. Doesn't that sound romantic?"

He tore himself away from Davis Love teeing off in a PGA match on ESPN and nodded his head. I'm willing to bet he didn't hear a word I said.

Oh, well. I can dream, can't I?

Closing my eyes, I pictured him pouring the champagne while we both mused over bits and pieces of our past. "Do you remember," I imagined him saying, "the priest who married us? He looked just like 'Radar' on *M.A.S.H.*, didn't he?"

My reply would be, "What I remember is you staring at him just before you burst out laughing! The man literally bounced on his heels waiting for you to get hold of yourself and say 'I do!' That's what I remember."

Babe, I am sure, will roll his eyes at that, like he always does. "Yeah, well, unlike you, nobody heard *me* giggle when it came time to say, 'For Richer or Poorer.'"

On second thought, maybe I don't want to imagine him reminding me of my little faux pax that day.

By the time the evening sun has set, the table will be laid out with good china, good silver and the bride and groom champagne flutes saved from our long ago wedding. I suspect by that time, the tapers would have gradually dwindled down to soft, waxy puddles and soft music will have floated poetic breezes our way, snuffing out the overgrown world just beyond our nest.

I plan to wear the same dress I wore on our wedding day, if it still fits. Babe will tell me I look prettier in it now than when I walked down the aisle. Bless his heart. I realize that getting him to change out of sweaty golf clothes and into something George Hamilton would wear will be a stretch, and I know bribery won't work. Maybe I'll just put out a pair of his good jeans and some clean underwear.

"You are more handsome than ever," I'll tell him, and he'll believe me because the truth will be reflected in my eyes. I ask you, when did clothes ever *really* make the man?

The two of us will be alone and content for a few precious hours. Joining us at different points during the evening will be memories we have created over the years, reminiscences that need no prelude or clarification.

I'm sure he will pour lots of champagne and he'll toast our weeks, months and years together. He may even tell me that he thinks often of the day we met. If he does, maybe I'll start humming, *The First Time Ever I Saw Your Face* to see if he frowns or begs me to keep quiet. And I, spilling over with champagne and romantic whimsy, will keep right on humming.

We won't bring up past disagreements. He won't talk about the dented fender on the new car and I won't mention the coffee stain in the middle of the living room carpet. Gone for a while will be any notion he might have that I don't appreciate him for taking out the garbage each night. Nor will I bring up all the times over the years I've prepared his favorite meals that went unacknowledged. On second thought, maybe I'll just mention it in passing. After all, we can't focus all night on those first *I can't live without you days* or we might not make it to the second course.

I am going to play a load of romantic CD's guaranteed to bring out the warm fuzzies because I know we will dance. We never pass up a chance to kick up our heels. Between courses, we'll waltz to poignant ballads, though not always with our feet. At times, we'll glide smoothly together with only a look to keep our inner music playing. (Sigh.)

If things go the way I hope, our anniversary celebration will evolve in layers, one course following the other. After too many sips of champagne and, with his tummy full of his favorite foods, he may have mellowed out enough for me to suggest a trip to Paris or Rome in the spring.

I can almost hear his response to that! "Maybe we'll go to Austria, too," he will say mockingly because he's thinking I have sipped way too much bubbly. Without a moment's pause, I'll simply counter with, "Or AusTRAlia," which will make him grin because he knows as I do, that it's all just a game.

We are old, Babe and me, although we don't feel it too often. I think we are still in love because we keep finding new things to like about each other. Okay, so he won't wear his Tux tonight. Big deal. In fact, he doesn't even have to change into the clothes I'll put out for him. And should he fall asleep while I'm tossing the salad, I'll just give him a swift, but soft kick and wake him up.

It's important for us both to remember that nothing can negate our experience of each other after all these years. Our feelings are as young as first love and as deep as a soul. What we have today may not be quite as fresh or filled with long-range dreams as when we walked down the aisle, but I'm betting that a little bit of that will surface tonight while we share good food and wine, slow dances and memories.

Babe and I will always need moments like these and we should grab them every chance we get before his bad knees or my bad back steals the slow shuffle from our anniversary waltzes.

> "If we can be the best of lovers,
> Yet be the best of friends,
> If we can try with ev'ry day
> To make it better as it grows,
> With any luck, then I suppose,
> The music never ends."

ZIP-A-DEE DOODAH

"It's the truth, it's actch'll, ev'rything is satisfactch'll."

THE DOODAH
SISTERHOOD

*"When women are depressed they either eat or go shopping.
Men invade another country. "*—Elayne Boosler

The Tuesday Doodah luncheon is already cooking with gas, in fact, the pot is about to boil over by the time I arrive.

"Well, hey, you. Kinda on the late side, aren't you?" Iris Nelle looks pointedly at her watch while hailing me with something akin to an authoritative, albeit ladylike voice. A Doodah never hollers like a piece of trash. A Doodah who was raised right, lifts her voice just enough to be heard.

I am huffing and puffing and nearly out of breath when I sink into the only empty chair I see. "I swannee, Frederica Road is going to make me late for my own funeral. I wish to my soul that the Yankee Snowbirds would stay put instead of coming down here tying up traffic."

Nobody hears me or responds, but I don't expect them to. We have an hour to talk about what we have to talk about before a "closed" sign is hung on the door of the cafe. After that, any leftover conversation is tabled until the following Tuesday.

Mary Grace and Ladye Gayle hold court week after week while sharing space at the head of the table that is located underneath a huge Elvis clock. Surrounding the two women are ten of us whose sole reason for being a Doodah Sister is our ability to say, "Bless Your Heart," whenever appropriate. However, not all of the Doodah Sisters are good ol' gals from the South who drop their "R's" and end their sentences with a preposition (i.e., "Where are y'all from?"). From time to time we add a token northerner or mid-westerner to our Salmagundi Bowl, but not before they have learned to love grits, okra and sweet tea.

I am seated in my chair trying to catch my breath when Kaytee, the most temperamental server on the island, saunters up to the table. She places a perspiring glass of the South's favorite beverage in front of me and then smiles. Kaytee takes good care of us when she's in the mood.

"Fresh white meat chicken salad today, girls. That's what you will order." A woman of few words, she figures out what we are to eat long before we arrive. She has a gift.

The Doodahs meet every week at this secluded cafe known primarily to Islanders who hope to keep it that way. Early on, we commandeered the Elvis Room in order to surround ourselves with autographed photos of The King in all of his glitz and glory. We grew up in the fifties and sixties and every one of us still mourns his death. The collectively projected awe within this tiny section of the cafe could not be more fitting.

"Hey, y'all," Nancy Faye's voice delicately lifts above the soft chatter. "I've got news. Robert Redford has had a face lift."

The silence is audible. Doodahs fell in love with Redford long before he got wrinkles. We bawled like babies for days when he dumped Barbra in *The Way We Were*. Not one of us is without a well-used video of that film. We like it so much better than *Butch Cassidy and the Sundance Kid*, preferring Redford—*our* Redford, past, present and future—sans facial hair.

"How's he look now?" Ladye Gayle asks with her hand over her heart, as though keeping it from jumping out on the table in front of her. Her face is frozen in expectation, her voice barely above a whisper. "Please tell me they didn't screw up his face."

A heartfelt sigh issues from Nancy Faye. "Let me put it this way. His shoes. Under my bed. Any time. Any day. Any night. Girl, he is so lookin' good."

Not only everybody seated at the table, but also even the table itself sags in mass relief. Paul Newman can age, Sean Connery can retire, homegrown tomatoes can whither and die on the vine. But not Redford. Not *our* Redford.

A chorus of "Thank the Lord" echoes throughout the Elvis Room as Kaytee returns with a tray of food heavy enough to kill a packhorse. In record time we are all munching like a bunch of goats while mouthing, "Mmmmms" and "Yums," as Kaytee expects us to do.

"Y'all hush up, now." Mary Grace stands up. "I'm fixing to make an announcement." She pauses until all the forks have been put down. "I just heard about a nutritionist in Waycross. He's supposed to be fantastic, and get this: He guarantees his weight loss program."

At once, the Doodahs become as silent as Trappist Monks. And then…

"Is that a money back guarantee?"

"Can we get diet pills?"

"Does he make you eat raw veggies and water sandwiches?"

"How much does he charge?"

Edna Earle, the oldest Doodah and long past her prime, never passes up a chance to invoke a sexual innuendo. "Will he take it out in trade?"

Mary Grace holds up both hands to stop the babble. "I don't know the answer to any of your questions, but I plan to go to Waycross so I can find out. I have either got to get rid of my love handles or get them registered as lethal weapons. If y'all want to go with me, then we'll caravan."

Ladye Gayle pops up with, "After we check out that doctor, then we can go to Ryan's and play The Field Hands Game.

Everybody looks at Ladye Gayle as though she's been sniffing nail polish remover.

"What on earth is The Field Hands Game," Julia Margaret asks.

Ladye Gayle grins. "That's when you pile food on your plate like a field hand. I hear they've got the best fried chicken in the entire Southeast."

A full chorus erupts around the table. "Count me in!" After that, we sit quietly for a moment, lost in a group fantasy of slipping into a Size Six bathing suit without first having to oil our bodies with Crisco.

"When do we leave?" asks Peggy Sue.

"Definitely not on Tuesday," say the Doodahs.

Good friends, good hairdressers, Robert Redford, Elvis and Tuesdays will remain firmly in place. Some things we will never change.

Making eye contact, we raise glasses of sweet ice tea and give the expected toast.

"Doodah!"

One Shoe Flew Over
the Cuckoo's Nest

*"Upon wearing high heels for the first time, the
girl noticed bald spots on top of men's heads."*—Author Unknown

Ladye Gayle and Mary Grace are determined to drag me off the island to go shoe shopping.

"We're going to Waycross, Georgia? Woo-Hoo! Can anybody tell me exactly when we got stuck in this 1960 time warp?"

Mary Grace turns to Ladye Gayle. "Po' thing. She just doesn't get it."

"I don't get what?" I feel a rush of stupidity surging through my brain.

Ladye Gayle clucks her tongue. "You've lived a sheltered life, haven't you, dahlin'? Tell us the truth. When was the last time you shopped for shoes?"

"Let me think about that. I'm pretty sure it was when Jimmy Carter was still governor, so that would be…"

Mary Grace blanches. "Ohmygawd! Ladye Gayle, the woman is pedi-impaired. We have certainly got our work cut out for us today."

They glance at each other knowingly, which makes me think I'm missing something important and I feel even more dim-witted.

"Why do we have to go all the way to Waycross for shoes," I chirp. "Let's just go to Pic 'n Pay in Brunswick. That's where I bought my last pair of thongs."

They stare at me as if I have just used up my entire vocabulary of four-letter words.

"Hush up and get in the car. You're even worse off than I thought. Thongs, for your information, are now sold in upscale lingerie shops, not in shoe stores."

Ten miles outside of town later, I'm still trying to figure out what's up with this shoe thing and why my two Doodah Sisters are tearing up Highway 81 as if it's the yellow brick road. They are practically giddy, and I've never seen anything like it in grown women.

Mary Grace is driving, doing eighty-five and pushing. Normally, she won't say a word while she's at the wheel, so when she speaks, Ladye Gayle and I both jump. "Y'all keep your eyes peeled out for the fuzz. One more ticket and Bucky says he's gonna cut up my credit cards, feed the pieces to the gators and ground me from now till kingdom come."

"How can I be a lookout, M.G. when I've got ten calls to return?" Ladye Gayle digs her cell phone out of a pocketbook the size of a Barcalounger and begins to tap in numbers. She cuts her eyes over in my direction and says, "You be the lookout. I'm way too busy."

Who me? How can I be a lookout when I can't seem to pull my eyes away from Mary Grace's speedometer that's climbing faster than Kudzu up a pole?

Ladye Gayle reaches her first caller and motions for us to be quiet. She is telling someone…lord only knows who…that she's on her way to the throat doctor and she's using a voice I've never heard before. She sounds like the Godfather.

"He's a E&T Specialist, you know. I'm praying he can do something about this awful sore throat of mine. Uh huh. I'm gonna try my best to be at work tomorrow for sure. Just take all my messages for me, if you don't mind. Okay?"

She flips the phone closed and laughs out loud. "I really should try to put my priorities in order. But this working thing just isn't working for me." She's dialing again before Mary Grace or I can begin to comprehend what she means.

We arrive at the shoe outlet in out-of-the-way, hard-to-get-there-from-here, God-forsaken Waycross, long before Ladye Gayle completes her ten phone calls. Undaunted, she sashays through the double doors of the store while still talking a mile a minute. I'm almost convinced that the cell phone in her ear has been surgically and permanently attached.

"What's that you say, Nancy Faye? You're breaking up. Oh Lord, I'm down to one cell. I'll have to call you tomorrow. Bye!"

"I've really got two cells left," she tells us with a giggle. "But good heavens! Why I should have to deal with Nancy Faye when I've got shoes to try on!" (She may well be talking about brain cells. At this point, I'm not sure.)

I watch in complete fascination as Mary Grace scurries down first one aisle, then another. With each step, her voice level rises until it is at fever pitch.

"Y'all! Come over here," she yells. "Quick! Look at this pair of shoes I've got on and tell me what you think. Are they to die for or what?"

I follow the voice that is bouncing off the walls and eventually find Mary Grace down on all fours surrounded by no less than twenty boxes of shoes. She snatches off the neon pink penny loafers, throws them over her shoulder quick as you please, then yanks open another box. She is in such a frenzied state that I barely recognize her.

"Mary Grace? Are you all right?"

She glances up briefly and I see a glimmer of recognition in her eyes. "I'm pretty sure I've died and gone to shoe heaven, so I guess I'm just fine. Where's Ladye Gayle?"

"Uh, I dunno. On the phone somewhere. I'll go look for her."

I find Ladye Gayle gabbing on her two cells while yanking shoes off the racks right and left. Her frenzy puts Mary Grace's frenzy to shame.

"I can't talk now," Ladye Gayle says into the cell phone. "I've got this awful stomach virus and I need to throw up right this minute!" Snapping the phone shut, she scoops up four pairs of shoes with her other hand without missing a beat.

"Ladye Gayle? Mary Grace is lookin' for you."

"Well, she'll just have to hold her horses. Tell her to call me on my cell if it's important. I can't stop now."

She slides both feet into a soft pair of Jimmy Choo's and within seconds begins to moan. Her eyes are unfocused and glassy when she looks up to say in a dreamy, sing-song voice, "I swear to my soul, I do believe I've find my 'G' spot. 'G' for Jimmy Choo. Get it?"

"Uh, I think he probably spells his name with a "J," Ladye Gayle, but don't let *that* put a damper on your moment of ecstasy."

Four hours and twenty minutes later, we are outside the store trying to figure out how to stuff one more box of shoes into Mary Grace's SUV without one of us riding home on top of the car. There's obviously not enough space for all three of us, let alone Ladye Gayle's Barca Lounger pocketbook. Worn to a frazzle, Mary Grace pushes hard on the side door of the SUV while perspiration spirals down her flushed face.

"Ladye Gayle, you'll just have to go back in the store and return some of those shoes you bought. That's all there is to it. If you didn't haul that humongous pocketbook around with you…"

A sudden hush drops over us as heavy as a wet Amish quilt. It's like everybody in the world stopped breathing all at once.

"Bite your tongue, Crab Cakes," Ladye Gayle hisses as she snatches out her cell phone and billfold, and then chunks her pocketbook and everything in it in the nearby trash can. Tossing her big head of hair, she announces, "Don't look at me like that. I am very good at prioritizing when I deem it to be absolutely necessary."

"You GO girl," Mary Grace and I shout in unison.

We heave ourselves into the SUV, cushioning our exhausted bodies among the mountain of shoes, way too many of which now belong to me.

Mary Grace tops her speed record going back home while chomping on a triple whopper with cheese and repeating over and over that she drives way too fast to worry about cholesterol.

Ladye Gayle has finally killed that one cell she's been lying about all day, and I sit quietly in the back seat admiring my new pair of thongs.

We all have our priorities

Calories Are Our Friends

"If I had been around when Rubens was painting, I would have been revered as a fabulous model. Kate Moss? Well, she would have been the paintbrush."—Dawn French

Mary Grace, Ladye Gayle, Babee Mo and I are taking our once a month trek to Weighcross. We have an appointment to see the Fat Doctor. Our Guru. Our Savior. Our tummy's Main Man.

"I've made up my mind." Ladye Gayle is fixing to rant. I can always tell because she turns off her cell phone and gets a facial expression that scares people into the middle of next week.

"I'm gonna tell the doc how Breyer's Ice Cream renders me powerless. I can't even walk down the frozen food aisle at Tweeters anymore."

Babee Mo yawns. "Awww. I can pass up Breyer's. But put one tee-ninezy teaspoon of Starbucks Chocolate Almond Fudge in my path, and watch me jump off the wagon, leap off the cart and pole vault off my diet. Now, *that's* what I call a problem, girlfriend."

As is customary for her, Mary Grace sits mutely behind the wheel. She's a self-proclaimed one-tracker and never talks when she's driving unless absolutely necessary. "I only do one thing at a time," she says. "Now, if y'all are counting on being around for a while, then don't distract me. You wouldn't want me to put a crimp in your long term objectives, would you?"

We usually pretend she's a hired chauffeur when it's her turn to drive. That way, we won't be tempted to talk to her and chance a much too soon conference with St. Peter. So today, when she suddenly pipes up with a comment, we almost kill each other looking for the quickest way out of the car.

"I think I have a computer chip embedded in my back molar," she announces. "It kicks in every time I open my mouth for any kind of food that tastes good."

Ladye Gayle, tightly gripping the door handle on her side of the car, is the first to speak. "A computer chip in your molar? You mean like Russell Crowe did in that movie, *A Beautiful Mind*? He was crazy, Mary Grace. Crazy! You ought not to go around saying things like that unless you want people to talk about you."

Mary Grace continues to speak in a singsong voice. "It's the weirdest thing. Nothing at all happens when I eat veggies. It's like that chip hunkers down in my mouth and takes a snooze when I'm crunching celery."

Mary Grace's SUV hasn't been this silent since it sat alone on the dealer's showroom floor. I don't know what the others are thinking, but two words pop up for me: shock treatments.

Babee Mo clears her throat. She has had more therapy than all of us put together so she's allowed to hold forth whenever there's a psychological issue at stake for any of the Doodahs. This appears to be one of those times, so we automatically look to her for a comment.

"That's understandable, Mary Grace," she says in a neutral voice so bland you'd think she was talking to a lamb chop. "Celery makes enough noise all by itself. It doesn't need a computer chip to speak for it."

I tighten my grip on the door handle. One more loopy comment and I am outta here.

Ladye Gayle hasn't taken her eyes off our heretofore-silent driver. "Russell Crowe saw imaginary people, Mary Grace. Do you see people, too?"

Mary Grace whips her head around and I begin to pray. Hard. She glares at Ladye Gayle and says, "So what if I do? What's wrong with that?"

Ladye Gayle's mouth is wide open and I can only guess that she's thinking the same thing I am. "Do those people make you draw pictures and stuff the way they did Russell Crowe?"

I feel lightheaded, like I have somehow fallen down the rabbit hole. Could they both be as goofy as they sound?

"What? Don't you believe me? Ladye Gayle, you're just jealous because I can see them and you can't!" M.G. sniffs before reverting to mute driving mode. I tear my eyes away from the door handle so I can look out the front window and what do I see? There is a vehicle ahead of us about a quarter of a mile. Mary

Grace sees it too, but instead of slowing down like any sane person would do, she floors it. We start to sail like the Flying Wallendas.

"Uh, Mary Grace? Are you nuts? That's a cop car in front of us."

"Don't talk to me! Can't you see I'm driving?"

"Uh, Mary Grace? That blue light up ahead is not advertising a K-Mart special. It's a vehicle equipped with sirens and handcuffs and guns and it has the word, "POLICE" painted from front to back and on both sides. Uh, you might want to slow down…"

She zooms past the fuzz like she's the frontrunner at a NASCAR event. I swivel my head around and catch the expression on the cop's face. It is not a pretty sight. I expect him to come tearing after us with his blue light flashing, howling that siren. But he doesn't.

Wise Ol' Babee Mo nods her head and murmurs, "We've got nothing to worry about. That man knows."

Ladye Gayle has not torn her eyes away from Mary Grace's jaw line since she started drilling her with those questions about Russell Crowe. It's as though she expects the intrepid computer chip to pipe up with the Gettysburg Address. I, on the other hand, am curious. "What are you talking about now, Babee Mo? The cop knows *what*?"

She lets out a turbo sigh and then, as though speaking to a small child, she says, "Four women speeding to Weighcross. Hello? He could stop us this close to reaching our goal, but he's smart. He knows better."

I am convinced now of my previous rabbit hole theory. "*What*, pray tell, are you talking about?"

"If that man keeps us from getting to Weighcross on time and we miss our appointment with the doc, he won't live long enough to spend his first Social Security check. He knows it, too."

We have "weighted" for a month to see the Fat Doctor. We ate enough celery stalks and carrot strips to convince Mary Grace that she's growing a computer chip in a back molar. We starved ourselves into near electrolyte coma. Should God be willing, and should the Fat Doctor declare a loss of even one pound, we will all be delighted Doodahs.

"Anybody up for eating lunch at Ryan's trough," I ask, even though I know what the answer will be.

Ladye Gayle says, "I never met an all-you-can-eat buffet I didn't like. Hey, Mary Grace, what does your computer chip have to say about that?"

Mary Grace doesn't miss a beat. "I don't much care what that thing has to say about it. But for the last couple of days, that annoying little girl dressed all up in an organdy pinafore and Mary Jane shoes, has nearly driven me up the wall."

I grab the door handle again and begin the count down. Ten, nine, eight, seven, six, five, four, three, two—one more goofy word, and I am so outta here!

Ladies and Gentlemen, Elvis Has Left the Building

"If life was fair, Elvis would be alive and all the impersonators would be dead."—Johnny Carson

Ladye Gayle is desperate, ready to get down on all fours and beg. "If you will let Elvis stay with you while I'm gone, I will reward you with a Botox coupon worth $300."

Didn't I say she was desperate?

Ladye Gayle is a vain, retro-fifties fanatic, which is why she named her cat in honor of The King. "Elvis Presley was the quintessential Cool Cat," she told me. "I am only doing my part to keep his memory alive."

"I hate to break it to you, Toots, but Elvis' memory doesn't need you. Every thirty minutes, Graceland slams the door on at least twenty Elvis fanatics who are hell-bent on keeping him alive."

Ladye Gayle wants to go to Atlanta this weekend and let a plastic surgeon liposuck the fat from her love handles and recycle it onto her lips.

"Puffy lips are sexy," she says.

Plastic surgery to Ladye Gayle is not medicine; it's a fashion accessory. I expect her to come home looking like her smackers have been inflated with a bicycle pump.

Her immediate problem is that there is no room at the Pampered Cat Spa for Elvis, and their wait list rolls over into the year 2010.

"I've got a cat of my own," I remind her. "As well as a dog. They reign. I'm afraid Elvis, king or no king, would have some difficulty with the pecking order."

"No, no, no, no, no! Believe me, Elvis's Alpha instincts deserted him light years ago. Please let him stay. It's only for one weekend. One tee-niney span of time."

"Okay, he can stay, but you owe me, Ladye Gayle. One Botox coupon won't even begin to cover it,"

Elvis is spooky. He hides in my closets and clothes hampers, under beds and even in my shower. He appears, as if by magic, only when it's time to bolt down cheeseburgers or peanut butter sandwiches. Now pushing twenty years old, he's thrived all these years on a diet straight out of Graceland. Before Ladye Gayle left town, she brought Elvis over, accompanied by a box of microwavable burgers and a lifetime supply of Skippy.

I attempt to mollycoddle the spoiled cat, but I am totally ignored. Then, the very first night when he goes out to do his business, he doesn't return. By midnight I fear the worst has happened so I shake the daylights out of my sleeping husband.

"Wake up, Babe. Elvis is gone."

He looks at me as if one of us is on hallucinogenic drugs. "For God's sake, woman. Elvis has been gone for more than twenty-five years. Go back to bed and sleep it off."

"Not THAT Elvis, Babe. It's Ladye Gayle's Elvis. He's disappeared."

"Cats are nocturnal, so quit fretting. Put a few burgers in the microwave and open the back door so he can smell them. He'll come back from the dead thinking he's been crowned the official Burger King. Har. Har."

"Bite me, Babe. I'm going out to look for him and you're going with me."

Babe opens one eye and stares at me with it. "Get real, girl. The only place I'm going is back to sleep."

"Not until we find Elvis, you're not. Now move it."

Armed with flashlights and ten recently microwaved burgers, we comb our own yard while Babe mutters words that I dare not repeat. My fear is that Elvis has been run over and is now flattened on the highway to heaven.

"Let's walk down the street and call out his name," I suggest. "He's probably disoriented."

"Are you nuts? He's a cat. They don't get lost and they don't get disoriented."

"I'm not nuts. I'm responsible. Turn your flashlight back on and start waving those burgers around."

Babe grumbles on his side of the street while I pray for the cat not to be dead, so I can have the pleasure of killing him myself.

"Elvis! Elvis!" I yell.

The expression on Babe's face changes into a snarl. He shakes his shoulders and drops into a really bad impersonation of Robert DeNero in *Cape Fear*. "Come out, come out wherever you are," he sings.

Two minutes later, he flicks off his flashlight and shoves the burgers at me. "I'm outta here," he announces, leaving me alone with two choices: either find the cat, or figure out how to tell Ladye Gayle that Elvis has left the building for good.

I continue to call his name when suddenly a hazy figure looms in front of me making me jump about fourteen feet in the air. When I land (like a cat) on my feet, I am eyeball to eyeball with an Elvis Presley look-alike who is gazing hungrily at the other Elvis' micro-burgers.

A deep, sultry voice says, "You gonna eat those?"

My mouth is hanging wide open when I hand over the hamburger booty as though it's a ransom.

"Thank you ve'y much," he says and takes a big bite.

"Who are you?"

"My mama calls me Elvis."

Yeah, right. It's after midnight and I'm standing on the street chit-chatting with a teenage idol lookalike. "What a coincidence," I say. "I'm trying to find a cat named Elvis before he becomes recycled Chinese Chop Suey."

He laughs. I half expect him to belt out, "He Ain't Nothing but a Hound Dawg."

Woofing down the rest of the cat's burgers, he motions me to follow as he strolls down the dark, deserted street. "I'll hep you find that ol' cat. I like meeting up with all my namesakes."

Five totally different strays answering to the name of Elvis respond to our joint beckonings. They trail along behind him as if he's the Pied Piper. When I check, none of the cats are wearing a rhinestone collar big enough to choke a horse.

Certain now that the cat has followed the real Elvis to junk food heaven, I thank the stranger and bid him goodnight. He gives me a mock salute, politely thanks me for the burgers, then shags off down the street. His rhinestone-studded outfit sparkles brighter and brighter with every receding step before he evaporates into the night. Or fog. Or haze. I blink and wonder if I have been walking in my sleep.

Ladye Gayle is going to come back with big, fat puffy lips and use them to spit poison darts at me. Even if I were to find an Elvis the Cat look-alike, how could I afford the wardrobe? She bought Elvis's rhinestone collar at Tiffany's. I'm not *that* blonde.

The house is dark when I return because Babe has left only night-lights burning. I'm feeling my way down the Hall when I step down hard on something soft.

Yeeeoooooooooooowwwwwww!!!!

It can't be Sophie Sorrowful who is sound asleep on the bed with Babe. It can't be ourTallulah Blankhead who's shaped like a Humvee, either. Stepping on her, would cause me to fall flat on my face. It must be Ladye Gayle's brat cat.

I click on a light just as Elvis darts away. I find him clinging to the chandelier in the dining room. He screeches when I reach for him, which brings Babe storming into the room hell-bent on killing an intruder. "I've got a gun and I'm not afraid of using it," he yells out with conviction.

"Oh, for god's sake, Babe. It's only Elvis. He's trying to hang himself on the chandelier."

"Shoot! I thought for sure I'd finally get to use my weapon. Freaking cat. I should shoot him anyway for waking me up in the middle of the night."

I sigh. "Let's just leave him alone. I know for a fact that he'll come down when he gets hungry."

Babe squints his eyes as he twirls the gun around on his index finger. "And just how do you know that?"

A sly smile appears on my face. "We won't go there, Babe. Let's just go on back to bed."

LIPS LIKE CHERRY WINE

"Where lipstick is concerned, the important thing is not color,
but to accept God's final word on where your lips end."—Jerry Seinfeld

It is Doodah Tuesday and Ladye Gayle has managed to capture the full attention of the sisterhood.

"Look at me. I put lipstick on a week ago Wednesday and you can see for yourselves, it hasn't budged."

She smiles broadly, showing off a row of teeth that appear (in contrast to her red lips) as white as Silver Queen corn.

Ten sets of eyes are fixed on Ladye Gayle as her tongue glides from one side of her mouth to the other, giving those ruby lips of hers a sudden, sodden gloss. "Is this to die for or what?"

"Put me down for three tubes." Mary Grace is digging in her pocketbook like she's looking for gold in them thar hills. "How much does it cost," she asks. "Oh heck, who cares? Just get me some of it quick as you can."

I look around the table to find Iris Nelle, Babee Mo, Nancy Faye and Peggy Sue also fumbling around in their pocketbooks, their heads wagging up and down in perfect sync like dashboard hula dolls. Two words, "Me too!" echo throughout the Elvis Room of our favorite hash house.

Ladye Gayle, on her recent trek to Atlanta for a monthly haircut and Botox revival, ran into a man on the street in a polyester suit selling something he called "Lip Stunner." According to him, when Lip Stunner is properly applied, it is as permanent as fingerprints.

Only two weeks ago, Sara Jane returned from Houston all agog over having had her eyelids, eyebrows and lips tattooed. She's been trying to talk us into doing the same thing, even going so far as to suggest that the Texas Tattoo technician would be willing to "do" us all in one fell swoop if we pay her airfare plus $800 per lid, brow and lip. Last I heard, the jury was still out with no plans to return a verdict anytime soon. That was one home improvement I didn't even think about discussing with Babe.

"Forget about tattooing," declares Ladye Gayle, then parrots what the man in the polyester suit told her. "Tattooing is too expensive and besides that, there's pain involved."

That, apparently, is the clincher. Within a few seconds, while talking a mile a minute and flicking her tongue over those crimson lips, Ladye Gayle is busy snatching up dollar bills faster than a carnie can give away free tickets to a peep show.

Babee Mo pulls out seven tubes of lipstick, along with a wad of bills fat enough to choke a goat. "Get a clean napkin, Ladye Gayle so you can smudge a sample of each one of these colors. Will eighty-five bucks cover it?"

"Do one for me, too!" giggles Peggy Sue. "I can't wait to wake up pretty."

I am unusually quiet as I watch our weekly luncheon get-together turn into the Home Shopping Network right before my eyes. I have a mental picture of a shifty looking guy with slicked-down, dyed black hair. He's wearing an apple-green polyester suit and chewing the kind of gum that won't stick to his dentures. In addition to peddling Lip Stunner he is happy to sell you a fake Rolex watch or a used car. "This baby is cherry," he brags. "Only driven to the liquor store and back once a week by a little old lady from Ludiwici."

I shake away the unbidden mental flashes because Peggy Sue's comment about waking up pretty has suddenly jump-started my motor. I may be somewhat past my prime, but I've never been a slouch. At my age, however, any effort to fool Mother Nature remains high on my personal priority list.

With that thought in mind, I pack up my brain and take myself on another mental trip, this time to my own dressing table where I pull open the cosmetic drawers that house my "urban renewal" tools. I'm shocked to discover no less than ten tubes of lipstick—Revlon, Elizabeth Arden, Clinique, Lancombe—and in some cases even Cover Girl. The possibility of my using them all up before rigor mortis sets in, is somewhere between zero and nil.

But wait. Maybe I'm missing the point. Lips that still blush after a six-course meal can't be all bad. Maybe I should reconsider having permanently rosy lips that pucker and plump and leave no telltale traces.

If I end up being eulogized because some huckster sold Ladye Gayle lipstick laced with arsenic, then so what? My stiff, white corpse will still be smiling behind lips the color of cherry wine, and the Doodah Sisterhood (should any of them survive their arsenic application) can all gather round my pine box and sing a chorus from the Flower Drum Song: *She Feels Prett-tee!*

Es Perfectamente
Absurdo!

"If you never want to see a man again, say:
'I love you, I want to marry you, I want to have your
children'. They leave skid marks."—Rita Rudner

Julia Margaret is determined to find the perfect man. She's even made up a list of the top ten essential attributes she hopes to find when she finally locates him.

He must love to cook and prepare innovative, impromptu meals (think Emeril without New York speak). She insists that he be eager to clean up any mess he makes in her kitchen (think Mr. Clean with hair) since she has no tolerance for dried food showing up on the Havilland china inherited from her grandmother.

Her man has to love poetry and enjoy reading it to her in a candlelit boudoir while sipping expensive, French bubbly.

"Poetry," she says, "is as much a requirement as his knowledge of current trends. By that, I mean knowing all about the 'A' list restaurants, diamonds, classical music and the ups, downs and pitfalls of Wall Street.

"A high I.Q.," she states, "is vital, but a sense of humor is only marginal."

Go figure.

I scan one of the two hundred fifty copies of her Xeroxed list, the one she's planning to post in every bar on every back road within a forty-mile radius of her house.

"Whoopsy" I hold up my hand. "You forgot something really important, Julia Margaret. You want him to be gorgeous and buff with lots of hair, don't you? What if he's a dead ringer for Lyle Lovett or Karl Malden?"

She gives me a look. "You can be so superficial."

"Well, then, shouldn't he at least be taller than you? Think about it…you're what? Five three? What if Mr. Bodacious sallies forth with every attribute on your list, but he's uh…height challenged? Like, maybe Danny DeVito?"

She gives me another look. "Are you trying to confuse me or what?"

I shake my head. "Not at all! I'm merely suggesting a few additions to that list of yours. The single women I know all look for a man taller than they are—with hair, although at our age maybe hair shouldn't be a huge priority. Then again, you're more likely to find a man over fifty with a good crop up top than one who reads Sylvia Plath to you in bed. Get real, girl."

She tosses her head and sniffs. "I prefer the Brownings. Robert and Elizabeth B."

"I hate to be the one to break it to you, Toots, but most of the men our age don't do poetry. They crawl under the covers, watch ESPN, fart, fall asleep and snore. Poetry readings in bed went out with Robert Goulet, Carol Lawrence and negligees."

She wrinkles up her nose as though catching a whiff of a passing garbage truck. "I have a rather large collection of negligees," she says before adding a sarcastic, "Thank you very much."

My mouth is a virtual flytrap. "You've got a negligee *collection?* You're not serious."

Her head dips to the left, and both brows lift slightly as she affects a wide-eyed, innocent ingénue expression. "I am so serious. Don't all *real* women buy negligees?"

I stare across the table at this person I thought I knew so well. If there is a Chronic Retro-fifties Syndrome, then this woman boasting about her peignoir collection must have a full-blown case of it.

Julia Margaret is a bit beyond middle-aged but still attractive. She works out every other day, drives around town in the obligatory pink Caddy presented to her by who else but Mary Kaye. She dresses to the nines and has taken every adult education class ever offered at the local community college. She rarely cooks, so that could be considered by some people as a negative. After tasting her infrequent attempts to emulate Martha Stewart, however, that would not be the case. (See: Perfect man requirements above.)

So what's wrong with this picture? Either she lives in a diaphanous world inherited from her mother, or she's a hooker with a client list of men over seventy years old. For all I know, she's a man who wears flimsy lingerie and pretends to be Loretta Young.

The last time Julia Margaret had a date was when her brother fixed her up with his recently divorced UGA roommate. Big brother slipped his old buddy fifty bucks and said, "Show my little Sister a good time, will ya? I gotta go see a man about a dawg."

The roommate, Hector was his name, took her to dinner at El Portro, bought her one Margarita (no salt) and said, "Eat your heart out, darlin'. It's all one price."

After pocketing the remainder of big brother's wampum, he waltzed her back outside to the pink Caddy. "I'm driving," he stated in a voice not to be argued with. She said "Okay," then watched in horror as he backed into the only other car in the parking lot.

Since Hector had downed three Tequila shots while Julia Margaret sipped her one Margarita (no salt) he was bound to top the DUI list. But self-preservation quickly kicked in and commanded him to spring out of the car like a Mexican jumping bean. Hector didn't think twice about shoving poor Julia Margaret over to the driver's side in order to assert his innocence if the cops showed up.

Not having had the advantage of three Tequila shots, the owner of the black Mercedes Hector had hit, was not a happy caballero. The front of his two-week-old luxury car looked like it had been driven up from Mexico that very day.

Julia Margaret has not spoken to her brother since.

I look at my friend's want list, and suddenly it hits me. Just like that, I understand where she's coming from and why that list of essentials is so important to her. Finding the perfect man is not what she's after at all. No! What she really wants is to find just one man who can wipe out her memory of Hector, the date from Hell.

"Uh, Julia Margaret? You misspelled gourmet in the first sentence," I tell her. "Correct that and make another two hundred and fifty copies, and I'll help you post them. Between us, we should be able to cover eighty-miles without breaking a sweat."

WRAP IT UP

*"Thank you for calling the Weight Loss Hotline.
If you'd like to lose a half-pound right now, press
one—eighteen thousand times."*—Randy Glasbergen

I have spent the last hour being measured and weighed. Presently, my body is wrapped in sopping wet ace bandages from the top of my head to my toenails. The process, according to Mary Grace, will make me skinny fast. As we speak, a big haired woman is squirting more foul smelling liquid all over me and she looks as though she is on a mission from God.

"It's minerals, Hon. They penetrate the gauze, seep into your pores and release ever one a them bad ol' impurities."

Personally, I'd just as soon let the bad ol' martini impurities stay right where they are, but my face is wrapped up so tight I can't talk. The Jaws of Life couldn't open my mouth at this point.

I roll my eyes far to the right and direct a look equal to a killer laser beam at Mary Grace, the Doodah Sister responsible for this afternoon of body torture. Actual tears are pouring down her face, which is *not* sealed tighter than a bag of Fritos because she didn't want to mess up her makeup. 'Don't touch my face,' she yelled.

Mary Grace is moaning horribly loud. "Uuuuhhhh! The grim reaper is standing in front of me grinning, the S.O.B."

"Nuuuhh uuuhh," I croak. "iiiissss ooooeee mmeeee."

Mary Grace quits sobbing and looks hard at what used to be me. "What did you say?"

Big Hair, looking slightly bored, sighs loud enough to be heard in Alaska. I bet she's wishing for it to be five o'clock somewhere in the world. I know I am.

Big Hair blows out another big breath. "Your friend said, 'It's her.'" She grabs more wet fabric out of a tub and begins to slap it around my hips. I figure underneath this gauze-soaked embalming fluid, I must be the color of a blueberry. I want so much to put my own clothes back on and get the hell out of Dodge, but every time I open my mouth, I sound like a helpless stroke victim.

Why on earth did I let Mary Grace talk me into this madness?

"We'll lose weight and inches all in one afternoon!" she promised. "Georgette said she lost fourteen inches her first time. Went from a size eighteen to a size six."

"Get out! What did she do, turn her body into human jerky? And Mary Grace, who is this Georgette person you keep raving about?"

"Oh, she's the owner of *Wrap It Up* and boy, is she is impressive."

"You've actually met her?"

Mary Grace squirms. "Well, in a manner of speaking I did. We kinda got acquainted over the phone." She squirms some more. "Well! She *sounded* nice."

Mary Grace's new best friend, aka Big Hair Georgette, is hovering over my helpless body and as much as I would like to, it would do no good to scream. Her accomplice, the one with the biggest butt in South Georgia, has stationed herself next to the only exit. I am convinced *that* is by design. If my mouth would only open, I'd offer both of them cash money to let us return to the real world while we're still alive.

Mary Grace groans again. It is a big groan and loud. I look at her out of the corner of my eye and see that she is way past ready to be humble.

"I'm begging you, Georgette," she whines. "Unwrap us and we'll leave quietly. We won't make a fuss. I promise. Just please, ma'am, don't hurt us anymore."

Ma'am? Did she just call Big Hair Ma'am?

Georgette's jaw is clinched even tighter than mine when she yanks my arm and motions for me to follow her. I am way too terrified to resist.

"Stand up straight," she yells. "Straight, I said! You look like a pretzel!"

I am shrink wrapped from one end to the other and she's telling me to stand up straight? I may kill this woman.

"Now, go on over to that rowing machine," she orders.

Who is she kidding? I can't even blink my eyes. Oh my God. Either we have wandered into AbuGhraib, or Big Hair is living out an Islamic fantasy.

Size Six Georgette grabs me by my other arm and drags my mummified body behind her. I have to follow but it's going to take hours. I look like Neil Armstrong in a space suit walking on the moon in slowmo.

My feet have been wrapped tight, and then covered in a baggie that's secured with a rubber band. My body impurities have collected inside the baggie and are squishing and sloshing with every excruciating step I take. That freaking rowing machine seems like it's three blocks away.

"Sit!" Big Butt Broomehilde borders the right side of me while Big Hair Georgette guards me on the left. If I don't do what they say, obey their every command, I'm afraid I'll never see Babe again. Mary Grace lets out another window rattling groan; she must be eyeballing the Grim Reaper again.

Once I get seated on the exercise machine, they order me to row in place for thirty minutes. My mind can only acknowledge two words: "in place." If I were buck nekkid, I couldn't row for ten minutes, yet these crazed terrorists expect me to do so while wrapped up like King Tut without his jewels. Help me, Jesus.

Suddenly, as if directed from above, nature pops up with the perfect escape.

"Aaaa haaa oooo eeee," I croak.

"Why didn't you go before I wrapped you?"

I shake my eyes back and forth. They're my only moveable body parts.

"Well, you'll just have to hold it."

"Nuuh uuuuhhh. Gaatta goooo ooowwww."

Number One Dominatrix glares hard at me and I am not ashamed to admit that I fear for my life. "You start unwrapping over there," she commands her sidekick, "and I'll have to undo this side, I reckon. Shee-it!"

Thank you Jesus.

While the two of them are trying their best to snatch me baldheaded, Mary Grace stops moaning long enough to yell out, "Me, too. I gotta go, too. I've got a tee niney bladder. Call my doctor if you don't believe me!"

It takes us ten minutes to become completely unraveled from the house of horrors but less than a minute and a half to gallop out of the door like Trigger and Buttermilk going after bandits who have just robbed the Wells Fargo stagecoach.

"Mary Grace," I yell through my clinched teeth. "I thought you said she was a nice person. Would you care to define nice?"

"I take it all back," she yells at me while frantically searching through her pocketbook for the car keys. "Every last word. Delete. Delete. Delete!"

I can't accept that. "Those women in there are crazy, M.G. Certifiable. I've never been so scared in my entire life. I thought for sure they were members of a cult and were trying to kill us. I could slap you upside the head for getting us into this."

Mary Grace cuts her eyes at me as a scowl forms on her face and her eyes turn black. "You touch this body in any way, shape or form, and I swear on everything that's holy, you will draw back a nub. Now get in the car and let's go home."

I know better than to argue when my nubs are threatened, so I do as she says. We are both silent until we are out of sight of the torture chamber. Mary Grace looks over at me and starts to giggle. It's contagious. In minutes, we are both laughing hysterically, so much so that tears are streaming down our cheeks.

"I need a Kleenex," she says and pulls the car over to the side of the road so she can look in her pocketbook.

"Ohhhh. What a day. Can you believe what we just put ourselves through?"

I shake my head. "Nobody will ever believe us."

She stops laughing immediately and grabs my arm. "Don't even *think* about telling anybody about this. You hear me? You say one word, and you are dead meat."

"Okay, Mary Grace. I promise I won't say *one word.*"

She has nothing to worry about because a column wouldn't be a column if it had only one word in it.

Heart and Shoe Souls

"A friend is someone who knows the song in your heart, and can
sing it back to you when you have forgotten the words.—Donna Roberts

When the Doodahs began to get together each Tuesday for lunch, our intention was to eat and talk about dieting; eat some more and talk about *not* dieting; eat even more and talk about shopping for shoes. Food equals energy and everybody knows that energy is a necessary commodity for a serious shoe shopper.

This sounds shallow and a bit silly to those unfamiliar with our group, but there is another side to us—a far bigger side. Beneath the surface of the Good Ol' Gal Guise we often wear, there lives a much deeper face that more aptly portrays our little bunch.

In the first Doodah year, we grew amazingly in heart and soul. Significant experiences occurred almost daily in each of our lives. While they were individually important, they were made even more meaningful when freely shared within our little cadre of lettuce eaters.

I remember it being a rather chilly and brisk day when Babee Mo waltzed into our annual winter birthday luncheon. Dressed to the nines, she was. Radiant. Casually, as if it were just another ordinary Tuesday, she said, "I gotta leave early because I'm getting married today." We pushed her out of the door ASAP and, with Libby Kate as her matron of honor, she became Mrs. Babee Mo, hitched at long last, and hopefully for longer than her other marriage, to her high school sweetheart.

A few months later, Mary Grace came to lunch and threw up her hands. "I've had it with mole crickets eating up the lawn and nasty old grubs chewing up my geraniums."

What's a Doodah to do, we asked in unison.

"I'm taking the plunge," she announced. "I'm downsizing, I'm purging. I'm getting rid of stuff. Condo City, here I come!"

Mary Grace had lived in a large, sprawling home for all of her adult life, so her decision not only came as a surprise, it scared us all silly. "How will you ever adapt to living in a condo," we asked.

"Oh, phooey," she said. "We'll do just fine." They sold the large home and bought the condo. Now when she serves us Escargot, we don't wonder (as we did in the past) whether the delicacy originated in her front yard or her back yard.

This year, Mary Grace's husband's cancer returned with a vengeance. As she began to center more of her activities on Sweet William, it became nearly impossible for her to lunch regularly with the Doodahs. We missed her ready smile, as well as her peppery sense of humor. Mary Grace and Bill were ever on our minds and certainly in all our prayers. But like so often happens when a devastating illness strikes a family, we were unable to make it all better for our friend. Mary Grace is a widow today and we look for every opportunity to help her through the grief. It is our gift to her, but we are very much aware that the gift is often in the giving.

This past summer, Libby Kate scared us all silly. She is a young looking sixty-ish woman with so much style it flows from her elbows. One Tuesday she announced in an off-handed way, that she would be checking into Mayo the following week. "I have to have a little surgery on my heart," she said.

We gasped. Not big as a minute, Libby Kate exercises regularly, eats so much rabbit food that she should have long floppy ears and a cotton tail. She hasn't come within ten miles of a pizza in ten years. In short, she is the last person on this planet you would expect to have a heart problem.

"It's nothing, really," she explained. "There's been a little glitch in my ticker since I was born, so my doctor said it's past time to fix it. Don't look so worried! I'll be out in plenty of time to go shoe shopping with y'all."

We planned the shopping spree for the week following Libby Kate's surgery, but fate is fickle. Family and friends were told that the surgery was successful, but that there was a slight complication. Slight? Only minutes out of the operating room, she experienced a sudden and totally unexpected coronary arrest. Libby Kate, we were told, was in a coma.

Talk about calling in favors! By sundown, we were phoning all over the country asking for her to be put on prayer lists, and for positive energy to be sent to Libby Kate as well as her family. I have always suspected that there was strength in numbers, but now I *know* it for sure. Today, our Doodah Sister is more vibrant and alive than ever before. It is impossible to look at her and not offer up a thankful prayer that she is once again healthy, happy and ready to have some fun.

Her first words when she came out of the coma? "Did I miss the shopping spree?"

It is safe to say that not too many chick clique years go by that we don't call upon our close friends to lend a hand, a heart or a shoulder on which to cry.

In our second year, Edna Earle came to us when her husband died after a long illness. She knew in her heart that Doodah friendship and love is solid, and that she could depend on us to help her through much of her sadness. And we did, just as we are doing now with Mary Grace.

It was like the time Peggy Sue needed our support when her grandson took sick. In no time flat, that child inherited more grandmothers than he knew what to do with. The day Peggy Sue heard that the test results showed Leukemia, she went next door to Glory Jean's and they did what Doodahs do when faced with heartbreak. They wept. They held on tight to each other. Then Glory Jean placed broken pieces of our friend inside her own heart, where they remained until the day the Doodahs newest grandson received a clean bill of health. That day came about not too long ago, and...well, there are no words.

While it is true that the Doodahs meet for lunch each Tuesday to laugh, gossip, and eat a lot of rabbit food, it has become so much more than chicken salad on Bibb lettuce. What we have together is a growing alliance epitomized by the caring and sharing that's always been more about feeding the soul than feeding the body.

On the other hand, a half decent salad bar has been known to make a huge difference in a Zip-a-dee Doodah Day.

ALMOST QUEEN FOR A DAY

Question: If you could live forever, would you and why?
Answer: "I would not live forever, because we should not
live forever, because if we were supposed to live forever,
then we would live forever, but we cannot live forever,
which is why I would not live forever,"—Miss America 1995

"I just don't know what I'm gone do without Bo Bo. Why, in my entire adult life, I have nevah even had to lick a stamp."

Glory Jean is whining because her husband of twenty something years took off with a nineteen-year-old hairdresser in the middle of the night leaving only a note.

"Glory Jean,

I'm through being your lackey, your bill payer, your flunky. From now on you'll have to figure out how to do your own nails, answer your own telephone and make your own hair appointments. You have done wore me out.

Don't bother to come looking for me 'cause I will be long gone by the time you read this. We are going to the island of Crete, where we plan to open up a cafe specializing in Southern food. Like, you know, Shrimp

Grits. I said "we" on purpose because Merleen will be going with me. Yes, Merleen from the Buck-a-Cut out on Highway 17 who has been taking care of my needs going on six months now, which includes cutting my hair. I know that some people might say she's a little bit young for me since she only graduated from high school last year, but doing hair is not the only thing Merleen has learned how to do. Unlike you, she taught herself how to cook.

I did a load of laundry before I left, put two quarts of my home-made spaghetti sauce in the freezer and bought two weeks worth of groceries that cost me way over a hundred dollars. You will have to figure out what to do next when the food's all gone and you don't have any more clean underwear.

Hasta la Vista.

Bo Bo"

Glory Jean is sitting across the table from me sniveling into a ragged Kleenex. Her eyes are rimmed in red instead of the overdone black eyeliner without which she normally would not be seen going to the mailbox. Her hair is flat as a flitter, a far cry from its normally teased and lacquered state. Glory Jean started back-combing and teasing it in 1960 and feels she mastered the technique. The fact that you could land a 747 on the top of her head has never seemed to give her a minute's pause. Her credo has always been: "Big hair defines who I am."

Ya think?

I place Bo Bo's farewell letter on the table and look up at the woman I have known for many years, but am barely able to recognize today. We go way back to the Sixties when Glory Jean was a professional beauty contestant. Her long-term goal was to win more Georgia competitions than anybody in the history of beauty pageants. Her mother, Dory Dean, stood behind her supporting her goal to the bitter end. I should rephrase that. Dory Dean pushed, shoved and cow-prodded Glory Jean all the way. Rumor has it that she took out a second mortgage on her house to pay for the designer gown Glory Jean wore in the evening dress competition at her first pageant.

She won a few and lost a few, capturing the titles of "Miss Butter Bean" and "Miss Savannah River Catfish." Glory Jean was even third runner-up in the "Miss Southern Railway System," no small feat for a South Georgia small town girl. She was a shoo-in to win the title of "Miss Water Nymph" over in Darien until an accident pulled the plug on everybody's odds-on favorite.

That fateful day, Glory Jean began her talent exhibition with a swan dive off the high board while wearing black patent leather spike heel shoes. I'm pretty sure nobody but me noticed the little splash she made as her feet hit the H20. She popped up out of that water with a smile on her face big as you please, flashing her whiter than white teeth which were shining brighter than a new porcelain toilet. She was on fire. Every strand of her lacquered hair remained exactly as it had been before she stepped off the diving board. Now that I think about it, a blowtorch couldn't have penetrated that mop of hair.

Her routine called for a water ballet, which she performed looking, if not like Esther Williams, at least like one of Esther's many fans. We all clapped and whistled as loud as we could while she shimmied up the ladder and out of the water for the final segment of her talent exhibition.

Shoulders back, tummy tucked, immovable hair intact and showing off her bleached molars with a smile leveled at the judges, she prissed herself over to the microphone clicking those spike heeled shoes. Glory Jean was supposed to serenade the audience with her chosen song, Handel's "Water Music," to which she had cleverly written lyrics.

A trumpet, a squeaky clarinet and a loud snare drum comprised the band hired to accompany her. In actuality, they were three discontented teenagers doing public service for over-fertilizing then setting fire to the school principal's prize winning camellia bush. They had almost finished the song's introduction when Glory Jean stepped up to the microphone with a veteran beauty contestant smile bonded to her face. Not realizing that she was also standing in a good-sized puddle of chlorinated pool water, she grabbed the mike as if it were the Miss America crown…Glory Jean's personal Holy Grail.

Glory Jean never danced that fast in her entire life. I can't even guess how much time passed before the audience realized that she was vigorously boogieing with enough electrical energy running through her body to power a small substation.

The kid playing the snare drum saw what was happening first and jumped up to unplug the mike. That was only after her mother, Dory Dean, began to holler, "You stop that carrying on right this minute, Glory Jean or you're gonna burn in Hell! Pentecostals ain't allowed to dance!"

As soon as the plug was pulled, Glory Jean's body collapsed into the chlorinated puddle she had made. Her hair, when that first spark of electricity got hold of it, still had not moved. When the voltage hit however, it went straight to her head causing every strand to stand up and say howdy. At that moment, Glory Jean looked for all the world like a deep fried Medusa.

She was rushed to the hospital where the doctors gathered around her while shaking their heads in wonder. None of them could understand why she wasn't dead or brain damaged, although if you ask me, it would have been hard to tell with Glory Jean. I am convinced that she owes it all to hair lacquer. It provided a protective shield and saved her life that fateful day in Darien.

Bringing myself back to the here and now, I look across the table at my friend and I clear my throat. "Ahem. Glory Jean, what you got to do is just forget about Bo Bo. He and Merleen deserve each other and you're better off without him. You're stronger than you think you are, so quit that whining and move on, girl"

She blows her nose and stares across the table at me. "So what is your point?"

"My point is that you don't need Bo Bo. There's a lot you can do all by yourself."

A turbo sigh shoots out of her mouth as though it were a field Howitzer. Cocking her head to the side, she folds her arms tightly in front of her. "Oh yeah? Name one thing."

I know she can't cook. Operating a washer/dryer, a no brainer for most people, makes Glory Jean break out in hives. Some people might say she's electronically, as opposed to electrically, challenged. I say she's spoiled rotten. Bo Bo did everything for her but chew up her food. She'd have trouble getting a job greeting people in the store where America shops. But I have to admit she *is* better than most at one thing: *Princessing.*

"Glory Jean, did you ever hear that old saying that goes, "Give people a fish and they eat for a day. Teach them how to fish and they eat for a lifetime?"

"I hate fish. Ever since my pool accident I don't eat anything that lives in water. I won't even get in the bathtub. If I can't get in a shower, I'll just stay dirty."

This is going to take longer than I thought. "Glory Jean, I want you to lean over the table and look at what I'm fixing to show you." I pick up a small scrap of paper and hold it directly in front of her between my thumb and forefinger.

"Now watch my lips," I say, before sticking out my tongue. "If you expect to survive in this world, the first thing you have to learn is how to lick a stamp."

A Witch for All Seasons

"There used to be a real me, but
I had it surgically removed."—Peter Sellers

Father Time is my beauty consultant. He told me (and I believe him) that a wrinkle is only an underdeveloped dimple. If one appears in a place other than on both sides of my smiling lips, I refuse to pay it the least bit of attention. Mary Grace, on the other hand, manages to catalog every one of my imperfections, no matter how inconsequential. It's as if she's on a mission from God.

"Did you make an appointment to see my plastic surgeon like I told you to do?" Mary Grace stands only inches from my face with her hands on her hips. Like an archeologist examining a minuscule bone particle, she squints her eyes and stares at my face.

"No, Mary Grace, I didn't call your doctor." I sigh dramatically. "Plastic surgery is like marriage…best not entered into unadvisedly or lightly."

She squints her eyes even tighter, the same baby blues that have been worked, reworked and overworked too many times to count. A bizarre noise begins to issue forth from somewhere deep inside her. I step away quickly, not knowing whether to throw up my hands in resignation or rummage around the room in hopes of finding a crucifix.

She shakes her head from side to side. "Did you forget to pay your brain bill or what? Time is not your friend. I'm telling you, you better do something about that face of yours and you better do it soon. One more summer in the sun and you'll be a Maxine clone."

I dig in my pocketbook in search of a mirror. "I don't look *that* bad," I say, getting more defensive by the minute.

She sighs with all the unprocessed drama of a high school senior playing Blanche in *A Streetcar Named Desire.*

"Read my lips," Mary Grace commands with a toss of her teased, sprayed and over-processed blonde hair. (She didn't get the nickname of Miss South Georgia for no reason.) "Your hair should be attached to a Halloween mask." She grabs my head and stretches clumps of my hair on both sides.

I admit my face might be starting to resemble a Virginia Creeper and it's probably past time I swapped Babe's rusty dog clippers in for a professional haircut. But a gal has to draw the line somewhere, right?

"Ow! Stop pulling my hair, Mary Grace. You keep that up and I won't be the only one in need of professional help."

Mary Grace's snide Halloween remark reminded me of a neighborhood teenage trick or treater last year. She came to my house dressed like that slut Gabrielle on *Desperate Housewives.* When I answered the door, she smirked and asked where I had bought my costume. I wasn't wearing one.

"Ooooh! Bree Van de Camp. You look just like her. How did you make up your face to be so, so, uhh...bland? And your dreary, unstyled wig...why, it's soooo perfect except like, you know, Bree's redheaded?"

"Uh," I interrupted her chant. "Wait right here a minute. My phone's ringing." I raced to the kitchen hoping to find something sharp and made of metal that I could bury inside her candied apple.

But back to Mary Grace of the multi-lifts. Since her last one, she sports a permanent smile plastered on her face as though she just discovered the multiple orgasm. What with her eyebrows tattooed three inches above her eyes and a transplanted widow's peak...why, even her grandkids don't recognize her anymore.

"Look," I say to my friend. "The truth is, Babe's got a problem with plastic surgery."

Actually, I haven't discussed it with him, but why not shift the blame? If I woke up every morning grinning like Clarabelle the Clown, Babe would likely become the Afghanistan Army's first American volunteer. Besides, I'm not dumb enough to grin before Babe has quaffed down his third mug of Starbucks. My mama didn't raise a fool.

Mary Grace's overworked eyes stare at me, a grotesque grin etched on her constantly smiling face. "Surely, you didn't ask Babe if you should get a face lift."

Clearly indignant, her recently implanted cheekbones turn into over-ripe tomatoes. Hoping for cheekbones not unlike Julia Roberts,' she took a little trip to Implants-R-Us. Unfortunately, she got Julia Child cheeks instead. You get what you pay for.

"Babe loves me the way I am, Mary Grace. When he wakes up every morning, he wants to recognize the snoring woman sleeping beside him."

Actually, what Babe said was, "When I was single, I was often amazed when I woke up in the mornings and recognized who I'd slept with the night before."

So I fudged a bit. So shoot me.

Mary Grace snorts like a horse, shakes her mop of bleached hair until it almost breaks loose from the three pounds of gel and hairspray.

"If what you say is true, then I have only one thing left to tell you." She sighs again with more melodrama than Julia Roberts could muster if her butt was on fire. "You should make friends with that teenage slut on *Desperate Housewives* before you answer the doorbell next Halloween. Otherwise, she'll recognize you."

"So what if she does?"

Mary Grace looks at me like I've been sniffing Babe's after shave. "Lord have mercy. Have you forgotten the trauma you caused that po' child?"

Tossing my limp head of hair, I sniff and try to look offended. "I did not put one thing in Gabrielle's apple. I only thought about it. There was absolutely no *trauma*."

"Then why did she hotfoot it down the street screaming about poisoned apples as if the Prince of Darkness had chased her out of your yard? Word gets around."

I fluff what's left of my bedraggled, unconditioned hair. Forcing a smile, I hope my unbleached yellow teeth will make the vertical lines above my lips appear a tad less noticeable. My untightened, tired eyes roll around in my head, and my oversized, hot pink nose twitches like a bitch-kitty.

"That television besotted bubbleheaded slut wannabee teenager needs to get a life and so do you. There is something to be said for natural beauty and growing old gracefully."

Mary Grace blows a lot of air through her puffy lips, rolls her too-tight eyes toward heaven and shakes her mop of bleached hair. "Natural beauty went out of style the day Hippies sobered up and invented computers and Clinique."

"What's a Clinique?"

"Ohmygawd. You're too far gone for even me to fix. Come on. Let's have a martini."

I'm out of the chair before she can move. Some things in my life don't need any repair. If a little tweaking around the edges should be needed, a dry martini, sipped slowly, has been known to make even undeveloped dimples disappear from sight.

THE FAMILY RESERVE

"Writers will happen in the best of families."—Rita Mae Brown

CHEW A LITTLE JUICY
FRUIT

"If we couldn't laugh, we would all go insane."—Jimmy Buffett

I read somewhere that a spokesperson for the American Dental Association announced that it could not make the teeth of the nation's citizens any damn whiter. That statement is a springboard catapulting me back to the day my niece married a dentist. I can see it clearly, as if it were that very day.

Babe and I are standing alone in front of an old Episcopal Church in Atlanta where, later in the day, the wedding is to take place. Having just arrived, we hope to catch a glimpse of the bride, as well as meet the groom before the "I do's" are said. We both thought the wedding party would have arrived by now, which makes me more than a little nervous. I am so trying not to bite off my recently acrylicked nails.

"Where could they be, Babe? You don't reckon the groom took to the hills, do you?"

"Naah. My guess is the entire wedding party is on I-285 looking in vain for an exit." He glances at his watch. "If they don't show up pretty soon, we'll phone for a helicopter and launch a Perimeter Search & Rescue Mission."

We arrived at the church early only because we got off the Interstate yesterday at the first Peachtree Exit. Why didn't somebody tell us that there are over a hundred Peachtree Exits in and around Atlanta? Realizing our mistake only after discovering areas of the city as yet unknown by modern civilization, we got back on I-285 and began circling the city for what seemed like many years.

Having lost last night's hotel reservations due to the unplanned Perimeter Excursion, the church sexton kindly allowed us to use the toilet facilities so we could tidy ourselves up a bit before the ceremony. The sexton became cooperative only after we convinced him that we were not vagrants bent on using up a month's supply of his paper towels.

"Babe, we must look like Country Come to Town. Here we are dilly dallying out here all by ourselves dressed up in our Sunday clothes." I look closely at him. "Did you know you've got paper toweling stuck in your whiskers?"

He yawns, scratches the private place where all men seem to itch. "Who cares? I told you we should stay in the car until we saw signs of life."

The truth is, I am no longer willing to sit next to Babe in the car listening to him polish off yet another pack of chewing gum. He has been jawing Juicy Fruit as if he's fixing to strike oil in one of his cavities. He somehow managed to chew the sweet out of four entire packs while we were doing circles around *Etlanna*. I so can't wait for him to kick the replacement habit that claimed his soul the day he gave up nicotine.

I am a ball of nerves. I cannot help but fear that this Mississippi fellow I have yet to meet has bolted back to the Delta without my one and only niece. And to think that she could have married my best friend's son, James Junior. He might not have a whole head of hair, and okay…signing up for a year or two at Weight Watchers wouldn't hurt him one bit. Just because a fellow is bald and overweight does *not* make him a bad person.

I shift from one foot to the other. I could kick myself for wearing new high heel shoes today. I am so involved with my numb toes and surrounding pain that I fail to hear the approaching gaggle of giggles. When I finally look up, I am taken aback by the approaching flock of females dressed in a whole lot of taffeta—all of them brightly beaming from their heads as though swaddled in strobe light.

I cross myself and quickly cover my eyes, praying that the light did not wreck my retina. "Babe!" I yank at his coat sleeve. "What's going on? I can't see squat! Can you?"

He's shielding his own eyes from the brightness of the swish gigglers. "It's too bright for me to see anything. Is this what they call hysterical blindness?"

"Don't talk stupid, Babe. How could we both become hysterically blind at the exact same moment?" I squint my eyes in hopes of focusing on whatever it is that's coming at us faster than sheet lightening.

"Holy Cow!" I exclaim. "I think it's a band of angels, Babe."

"What are you talking about," he asks. "Did that bright light cook your brain?"

"If they're not angels, then they're human flashlights." The Biblical story of Lot's wife darts through my mind making me recoil in terror. Squeezing my eyes completely shut, I turn my back on the approaching light and dare not look around.

Chill bumps run up and down my spine. I sense a close presence, then feel a tap on my shoulder. The voice of my only niece breaks the spell I am under as I slowly open my baby blues and turn around. She and her bridesmaids are staring at Babe and me as though we are in need of immediate intervention.

"Whatch y'all doing standing out here all by yourselves? And what's up with the closed eyes?" She gives me one of her amazing smiles and that's when the light dawns, both literally and figuratively.

The soon-to-be groom/dentist has bleached the pearly whites of my beautiful niece. Not satisfied with the one mouthful of whiter than whites, it appears that he has also done a Clorox number on the bridesmaid's teeth as well. Bless their hearts, they just can't help showing off those Chicklets. Collectively grinning, they could light up a small country. I am sure of it.

Babe is working furiously on the last bit of sweet in his most recent wad of Juicy Fruit when I poke him in the ribs. "Better fetch our Ray-Bans out of the car, honey. Looks like we're gonna be needing them for the rest of the day, into the evening and long after the fat lady sings."

WHISTLE A HAPPY TIME

*"Old as she was, she still missed
her daddy sometimes."—Gloria Naylor*

Having taken its own sweet time, autumn has arrived in some parts of the South. This annual materialization of nature never fails to make me nostalgic. When the sun begins to drop behind buildings more quickly each day than I want it to, I find myself looking out through the windows of my past and thinking about my daddy.

It is late afternoon, mid-October. A cool breeze drifts down to settle for the night in the small South Carolina town while I chat with my girlfriends. I first notice the nip in the air when my fingers don't bend the way they did an hour before. Smoke climbs over the rooftop at the Brantley's house making my nose sting from the pungent smell of burning leaves in their back yard. I don't mind it. Like other everyday things that I scarcely notice, the smell, the nose-sting, even the smoke, they all occupy a rightful position in my young life.

Across the street, my friend Linda dutifully sweeps the driveway. Her daddy is raking leaves and stuffing them in a wire mesh basket to be burned later. Saturday morning, perhaps, while he is off from work and his teenage boys don't have football practice.

My girlfriends and I talk about everything: homework assignments, the cute boy who moved to town from Charleston, the hot, new lipstick color, the penny loafers Mama just bought me or the Sadie Hawkins Day Dance coming up on Friday night after the football game. We take turns talking, but we never seem to get it all said. We flap our hands a lot.

Normally, about this time of day, I hear the sound to which I've been unconsciously listening. No, it's not the ring of a cell phone interrupting our scatterbrained girly conversations. It is much too early in the century for microchips and fiber optics to begin governing our lives. Most families have only one basic black telephone with no dials and no touch-tones. My folks don't even allow me to use the phone until I've practiced the piano for an hour and have finished all my homework.

Upon hearing the anticipated sound, my girlfriends and I immediately stop our talkfest and hand gesturing. We stand poised and listen for the second sound soon to follow. Sure enough, it does.

It's Daddy's whistle. Time for me to go home.

"Gotta go," I say quickly as I jump on my bike and peddle down the street toward my house. I look back once at my girlfriends to see them wave as they keep right on talking.

Like all the other fathers in our neighborhood, Daddy has a unique whistle used only for calling my brother and me to come inside. He puts two fingers in his mouth, presses down hard, rolls up his tongue, then blows through his fingers. The sound he makes, "whew-ah-whew" has its own timbre, slightly rising as it reaches its final "ah-whew." It is not a quiet whistle. In fact, it is loud enough to be clearly heard two blocks away.

I recognize other whistles from other fathers, but it is my daddy's unique sound that I respond to as fast as I can. He whistles only twice, allowing a full ten minutes for my brother or me to finish what we're up to and come home to get washed up for supper. Both my brother and I have better sense than to ignore Daddy's second whistle.

The crisp autumn weather has put Mama in the mood to make a pot of chili and a full steamer of rice. (South Carolinians seldom have a meal without rice.) My brother and I drink milk with our supper, milk left at our front door in quart bottles before the morning sun came up. Any chili remaining in our bowls is quickly sopped up with thick, crusty home-baked bread, lathered with Aunt Polly's country butter, that sweet, slightly sour taste that Parkay can only dream about.

After supper, Mama and Daddy go into the living room where they read the day's newspaper. My brother and I are relegated to the kitchen where it is our duty each night to wash and dry the dishes while trying not to kill each other.

It is a ritual, this evening regimen of our little family. It is the way we close the door on another day. We say grace before eating supper together; my brother washes the dishes and I dry; Mama and Daddy read the paper but don't talk much. All of it begins with Daddy's late afternoon whistle.

No doubt today's cell phones are a far better form of communication between parent and child, if one doesn't forget to keep the batteries charged, that is. But nothing can ever replace the warm feeling that overcomes me when my nose starts to sting from the smell of burning leaves, or when I dig into the humpback trunk for a sweater to ward off a sudden afternoon chill. I feel it in my soul when it's time to cook a big pot of chili or when a nip in the air tells me to take off my sandals and put on socks and real shoes.

This is the time of year I find myself longing to hear that special, unmatched sound that came from my daddy's lips. I wish I could go back to those times and let him know how much that small piece of everyday life means to me now. I want to hug him as hard as I can and say, "I remember how you used to whistle for me and how it always brought me home."

Who Was That Masked Man?

"When confronted by a difficult problem,
you can solve it by reducing it to the question,
'How would the Lone Ranger handle this?'"

Some time back, I asked Mr. Breedlove, a professional photographer I have known all my life, to restore and enlarge an old photo of Mama and Daddy. Today, he stands before me having just handed over the results of his meticulous work. He is preening like a Texas beauty queen.

"It's simply beautiful," I exclaim. Then I slip on my up-close glasses to look at it in more detail.

I gasp. "Mr. Breedlove? Who is that man?"

"Why, it's your daddy." He peers over my shoulder. "Idn't it?"

I shake my head. "Mr. Breedlove, I have no idea who that is. I thought it was Daddy because of the hat, but now that you've enlarged it and all, I see that it's not. I've never laid eyes on that man."

I keep staring at the beautifully restored, hand-colored portrait of what I'd always believed was Mama and Daddy. "He looks vaguely familiar. Kinda like a cowboy, don't you think?"

"Lemme see that!" Mr. Breedlove snatches the photo from my hands. I am so confused that I don't get all huffy about his obvious rudeness the way I normally do.

Holding the 10 x 12 enlargement out as far as his arms will stretch, Mr. Breedlove doesn't just look at the picture, he glares holes in it and his mouth drops open. If I didn't know better, I'd swear he is witnessing the Second Coming.

"As I live and breathe," he mutters in a tone akin to a prayer. "I know who this is. It's the Lone Ranger."

I snatch the photo out of his trembling hands.

My mother was a good looking woman, still turning heads way past her 70th birthday. Daddy was nice looking, too, but where Mama was photogenic, Daddy couldn't take a good picture if his life depended on it. I quit looking at him in photos long ago, preferring to remember him as he really was rather than the proverbial deer caught in the headlights.

I suppose that must be the reason I never paid any attention to that stranger standing next to my mother until Mr. Breedlove brought me the enlarged photo. The original was very small and badly wrinkled and yellowed with age. And, my eyes are bad and getting worse.

I blink a few more times before peering again at the photo. "Holy Cow! I can't believe I never noticed this."

Mr. Breedlove jumps up like a frog in a Mark Twain tale. "What? What? Did you see somebody else? Is it Tonto?"

"Calm down, Mr. B.," I say quietly, hoping the tone of my voice will be powerful enough to make him do just that. "Before you start thinking about calling the National Enquirer, you need to majorly chill."

He looks deflated and a bit confused.

"There is nobody famous in this photograph, Mr. Breedlove. Not the Lone Ranger and not Tonto. Not Roy, Dale or Trigger, either."

"Then why did you yell 'Holy Cow!' like that? You got me all jiggy."

Dear Mr. B. looks like he might be fixing to have a wee stroke.

"I'm sorry I yelled," I say hoping to calm him down before I have to call 911. "Look at the man's eyes and forget about the hat. The eyes are hooded with dark circles underneath them. That's what makes him *look* like he's wearing a mask."

"It's him! It's him! I tell you!" Mr. Breedlove jerks the photograph away from me again and begins to study it as though it's a sterling silver bullet.

This yanking back and forth is making me dizzy.

Shaking his head like a wet dog, Mr. B. declares, "He's masked all right, and that is very significant, if you ask me."

My first thought is that he's *got* to be kidding. My second thought is that Mr. B. doesn't know *how* to kid. He never did. The man laughs even less than a Republican.

I take a deep breath and smile as though his exclamations make even a grain of sense, then I slap my forehead and feign a Eureka!

"Oh my Lord! It's all coming back to me now. I know who that man is!"

"You do? Is he somebody from the *other side?*"

I fake a laugh, but Mr. Breedlove is starting to scare me. I wish I had the nerve to tell him to ease up on his caffeine and stop watching late-night TV. "The other side? Naaah. Nothing so intriguing and exciting as all that!" I reach over and gently take the photo from his shaking, clammy hands.

"It's my Uncle Mac, my mother's step-brother! I didn't recognize him right off because I only met him once when I was a little girl. He lived off the Louisiana coast on an oilrig. He didn't much like people, Mama said, and he only came to see us two or three times. Shoot! I forgot all about him."

Mr. Breedlove looks like I have just snatched away his one reason for living. He purses his lips, raises an eyebrow and sniffs. I am not at all prepared for what comes out of his mouth next.

"You didn't have to lead me on like that, missy. I am a well-known professional and I don't appreciate being the butt of one of your jokes."

Just wait till he reads the column I'm going to write, I think to myself.

"Now, Mr. Breedlove, you have known me for a lot of years. You don't really think I would do something like that, do you? I am just as shocked as you are to find Uncle Mac's grinning face in that photograph instead of my daddy."

He grumbles and mumbles to himself while I lead him out to his car. If he's going to pitch a hissy, I do not want to witness it.

"Thanks again, Mr. B., for your beautiful restoration. I only wish Mama could see it. She would be so proud." I might just as well be talking to the taillights of his car. He sticks his nose up in the air, directs his eyes toward the street in front of him and drives off in a huff. I wave goodbye. He does not wave back.

I slam the front door, snatch up the picture and stare harder than ever at it. Who on earth is that masked man standing next to my mama? Lord knows I don't have a clue, OR an Uncle Mac.

ART IMITATING LIFE
IMITATING ART

"I was to think of these days many times. Of Jem and Dill and Boo Radley, and Tom Robinson and Atticus. He would be in Jem's room all night, and he would be there when Jem waked up in the morning."
—Harper Lee, To Kill a Mockingbird

It is early February 1962 and I am curled up on the sofa with a book. A crocheted afghan covers my knees and protruding belly. A forgotten pot of tea on the coffee table gets cold while I get lost in Harper Lee's Pulitzer Prize winning novel, *To Kill A Mockingbird*. The book has me laughing out loud one minute, then crying softly. Even so, I don't want to put it down. In fact, I can't turn the pages fast enough.

I am to become a mother within the next few months and the antics of the young characters, Jem and Scout, have snatched my heart and tickled me to death. Setting the book aside for a moment, I allow my eyes to focus heavenward. *God, please help me teach my child to be as delightfully mischievous as those two scamps. Amen.*

I am filled with admiration for the father of the two rascals, Atticus Finch, the principled attorney courageous enough to stand up for what is right. I am inspired to again ask God to help me instill strong principles in my unborn child.

*   *   *   *

February 2003:

Road stressed and ragged from driving alongside too many big rigs in awful weather, Babe and I arrive at a Charleston hotel and drag our weary butts into the lobby.

Tornado warnings had trailed behind us all the way from Georgia, but fortunately Babe's NASCAR wannabee persona kicked in just in time. In what seemed like a nanosecond, he changed from a law-abiding citizen into a crazed racecar driver determined to outrun the funnel shaped cloud. Sitting mutely in the passenger seat beside him, I gripped anything grippable and tried not to destroy my manicure. The moment I stepped out of the car, I unabashedly kissed the rain-soaked South Carolina ground.

We check into the hotel and as quickly as the technicalities can be resolved, forms signed and key cards assigned, we hightail it up to our haven for the night. The last three grueling hours on the racetrack from Hell have left me with a monster of a migraine that is trying mightily to kill me. Consequently, in less than thirty seconds I dive head first onto the bed and close my eyes.

Late in the afternoon, we meet my oldest son for dinner. The rain has stopped, thank you God, and since the small French restaurant is located near the hotel, we take off on foot. After downing a double martini and a beautiful dinner, I feel almost myself again.

By eight o'clock, we are in our seats near the stage at the historic Dock Street Theatre awaiting the curtain. Tonight's special presentation is none other than the stage adaptation of *To Kill a Mockingbird*. It has been over forty years since I lay curled up on the sofa reading the book (for the first time), feeling very pregnant (for the first time), and feeling very scared (*not* for the first or last time). As fate would have it, I am now seated next to the very child I was carrying at the time. The synergism does not escape me.

So much has happened since 1962.

Our country fought a war and lost, then fought another war and claimed victory. We had our hearts broken by the assassination of one president and the deaths of two others. Another of our country's leaders left the Oval Office and became an even greater influence while living his dream of making life better for those who had suffered too much already. We even survived a president who was bent on disgracing himself as well as the nation, and we managed somehow to live through all the turmoil created out of his misguided actions.

There was a shuttle explosion that ripped through the souls of all Americans, then another more recent one that left each of us once again heartbroken and bereft.

In forty years, we have lived through tragedy and grief, and we have survived. Even 9-11, as unthinkable as it was to our people, served to make us more cognizant of the precious gift of life. It reminded us all that lives are fragile and can be snuffed out in the blink of an eye. A sad, tragic reminder, but one we are all forced to live with each and every day.

A country can only be as strong as its people. Individually, we make America what it is. Collectively, we hold the model tools for other nations: tools of patience, generosity, acceptance, tolerance and above all the keys to global peace.

With all our many advantages and all the ups and downs we have experienced, there seems to be a missing yet essential ingredient vital to the souls of our people. We need something more than the things money can buy and I have an idea what that something might be.

We need more people like Atticus Finch who are willing to sit up all night with an accused man because rumor has it that vigilantes intend to do him harm.

We need more people like Atticus Finch who will recognize a moral injustice for what it is and will do what is necessary to right the wrong.

We need more people like Atticus Finch to question the status quo if and when it no longer works for everyone in their community, their state or their country.

We need more people like Atticus Finch who take enough time with their children to become heroes to them again and earn their respect.

We need more fearless people like Atticus Finch, who are willing and eager to think outside of the box, and who are unafraid of what others may say or think.

We need more people like Atticus Finch to believe in the basic goodness of us all, to give honor to others regardless of race, color or creed.

We need more people like Atticus Finch.

*   *   *   *

As I leave The Dock Street Theatre, my mood is more somber than when I entered. Walking at a leisurely pace down Dock Street on this cold February night with my first-born son at my side, I am so aware that life lessons experienced and studied over the past forty years have not been lost on this fine young man. As we walk, I allow my eyes to focus heavenward.

Thank you, God, for helping my son to become the kind of man I always hoped he would be. Thank you for showing him the tools to use as a small-town attorney who resonates with integrity and decency because God, this world needs more people like Atticus Finch. Amen.

If I Could Sit On The Porch With You

*"I believe that what we become depends on
what our fathers teach us at odd moments,
when they aren't trying to teach us."*—Umberto Eco

"If you had the chance to sit on the porch in a rocking chair," my friend Beverly said, "and have a long visit with someone living or dead, who would it be?"

John F. Kennedy crossed my mind, as did Eleanor Roosevelt and Anne Morrow Lindbergh. I would give up an eyetooth to talk with any one of them.

Yet, after thinking about it some more, the person I chose was not famous at all. He did not find a cure for any disease, never wrote a book, nor did he do much of anything to distinguish himself outside of the small town in which he was born. Given what he had to work with, however, he accomplished a lot.

The man I chose was my daddy whose life ended much too soon.

"There are two things I hope you will always remember, honey," he said to me. I had been married almost a month when he came over for a visit. "Number one," he held up his index finger, "never, *ever* buy plain hamburger meat in the store."

"Why, Daddy?"

He sighed. "Because the butchers take the unmentionables and grind them up, add some fat to it and call it hamburger. Trust me. You don't want to put it in your stomach."

When Daddy was first married, long before he got into police work, he got a job as a salesman for a meat packing plant. That was right after the Great Depression, before the FDA began cracking the whip in super markets. No matter. The sight of cow parts being prepared for human consumption was a vision burned onto the walls of his brain. For all the years I knew him, I never saw Daddy eat a hamburger.

"Okay now, the second thing you need to remember," he said, "is this: your coffee will always taste better if you drink it out of a thin cup."

Since I was a young bride at the time, I was actually hoping for sage advice from my parent. I thought he might give me hints about balancing the budget or keeping love alive in a relationship. So what did I get? My Daddy, serious as a heart attack, enlightened me with a complete list of stomach-turning ingredients found in hamburger meat. As if that were not enough, he then counseled me to drink coffee in a thin cup. I just didn't get it. I kept right on drinking Maxwell House Instant in the thickest mug I could find, the kind that would not break if I threw it at my husband because Daddy had not thought to enlighten me with the secrets of keeping love alive.

It was years later before I discovered the pure satisfaction that comes from a cup of coffee brewed with fresh ground beans imported from Colombia. Not until then did I find that the taste could indeed be enhanced when poured into a thin china cup—one I could almost see through.

My memories appear to be strange, inconsequential conversations with my father. But what might we talk about today, I ask myself, if the two of us were sitting, as my friend imagined, in two rocking chairs out on my screen porch? What would we think to say to each other while watching egrets fly overhead and listening to a dog barking somewhere in the distance?

The first thing I would do, I think, is pour us both a cup of freshly brewed, steaming Starbucks French Roast into a bone china cup, of course. I would add a splash of half and half to mine while Daddy, being the coffee purist, would shake his head in disapproval. "I thought you had better sense than to taint a good cup of java with milk," he would surely admonish.

Then, I think I might take Daddy's hand in mine and simply hold it for a little while. I would try to memorize the shape of his long fingers while running my own fingers, formed so much like his, over his knuckles, his nails, his FBI Academy ring. I would carefully examine both sides of his hands while trying to recall whether or not my children's hands look anything like my father's.

After a few minutes of quiet time, I might say, "Daddy, what do you regret NOT doing while you were alive?" Secretly, I would hope he'd say, "I regret not hugging you kids more or loving your mother harder." Most likely he would reply, "I regret not catching that SOB who robbed the First National Bank!" But, maybe not.

I would want to tell my Daddy that, in spite of everything, all the missed opportunities that lingered between us for years, I had loved him deeply. Beyond that, I respected him for what he was able to accomplish with no formal education. I would tell him how much I admired his willingness to take responsibility for our town's safety, even if we as a family were too often shortchanged in the process. (Maybe I wouldn't bring that last part up.)

Finally, I would ask him to put his arms around me and hold me for a few precious minutes. I'd ask him to be my daddy again for a while. I would say, "Let's pretend that all the years have *not* gone by, and that I'm still your little girl."

How might I assure him that he was a very good man while he lived, that his family was proud of him and the difference he had made in so many lives? How might I tell him the things I never told him? Maybe I could start with, "You were really important to me, Daddy, and I loved you so much. I wish we had been closer. I wanted you to hug me, but you never did. I can show you how to hug now, if you want me to."

I would try to say something funny to make him laugh so I could burn the vision of his smiling face onto the walls of my brain. That way, I could carry it with me until I get to that all-you-can-eat, artery clogging hamburger buffet in the sky.

Dolly's Memory Trunk

"The best thing you can give children, next to good habits, are good memories."—Sydney J Harris

It was only a handkerchief. White, edged in tatted lace and yellowed with age. It was small, created for a lady to stuff in her pocket or inside the sleeve of her dress. I found it one day while rooting around in an old trunk that had once belonged to Babe's mother.

A bare light bulb swung back and forth from the attic ceiling illuminating only a portion of the trunk as I opened the lid and listened to its lingering creak. Brittle snapshots fell away from flat-black pages of old scrapbooks; torn newspaper clippings baked to yellow parchment, shredded into tiny pieces at my touch. I found Babe's confirmation certificate in that trunk, a pair of his bronzed baby shoes and his First Grade primer, *Fun With Dick and Jane*.

"See Spot Run? Run, Spot, Run!"

Digging even deeper, I saw a box and picked it up. When I opened it, the fragrance of roses floated up to me and made me smile. Babe's mother's passion for roses was legendary. "It's genetic," Babe told me. "She inherited it from her mother." Inside the small box lay a dainty handkerchief also yellowed around the edges and pinned in place so as not to get creased. As though it had a will of its own, a folded sheet of paper fell out and landed in my lap. I picked it up and began to read the elegant penmanship.

"Hello!

If you are reading this, then you must be my son's wife, the daughter-in-law I never knew. Somehow, you have found your way up the long attic stairs and are sitting on the floor (I hope) picking through this trunk and wondering what on earth it all could mean.

So! The first thing I should tell you is that the trunk and all of the contents now belong to you. I want you to have it all. I am leaving notes on everything for one reason only: so that you might get to know me a little and learn something about our family. Everything in the trunk was important once. Not just to me, but to all of the family. I see it as a patchwork quilt of our lives. You are family now, and that is why I want you to be the one to discover what still lives inside this trunk.

"The handkerchief you are holding was given to me by my mother on my wedding day. It had also been her wedding handkerchief as well as her mother's before her. Unfortunately for me, the loving words of wisdom that came with the handkerchief were lost in the ebullience of my wedding celebration. Many seasons had to pass before I would remember her words.

"I was very young and so much in love on my wedding day. I knew nothing about married life. Nothing! In my young mind, I pictured myself cooking our meals all dressed up in my best clothes. I saw myself serving them to my family without ever burning the toast or over cooking the roast. I was so convinced of my made-up married lifestyle that my mind would not allow me to imagine anything could ever change it.

"Being in love was wonderful and I wanted us to stay that way forever and ever. How naive I was, how completely unprepared for reality. How tragic I was to feel later.

"My mother's words came home to me one cold winter day as I rocked young Babe who was slowly recovering from pneumonia. He had been so sick and I'd been worried half to death. Although I needed a good cry almost as much as I needed to breathe, it was not until the restless boy finally fell asleep that I allowed myself to break down.

"Without having to even think about it, my left hand dug down into my pocket for the handkerchief I always carried there. It was at that very moment when my mother's words, spoken to me on my wedding day, all came back to me. She said:

'This handkerchief, dear child, will wipe away your tears on days when you feel your heart will surely break, when you feel unloved or simply taken for granted. It is yours for the times you sit alone recalling your past loves and wondering what if? What if?

'This handkerchief is for when you feel new life growing inside you and somehow you understand that the tiny being you feel embodies all the love you hold in your heart. It is for when you hear your child gasp his first breath, when you count his tiny fingers and toes, when you hold his little face close to yours so that he might taste your tears. You'll laugh till you cry the day your baby says Mama for the first time, and you'll shed compassionate tears when he falls off the sliding board and comes running to you for solace and a Band-Aid.

'You'll cry like a baby on his first day of school. Your heart will break when he doesn't make the team, when his first love doesn't give him a valentine, but the neighborhood bully gives him a black eye. These are only some of the things that will surely render you sleepless, but it will be nothing compared to the anguished nights you'll spend when he leaves home for good. The sudden silence in every corner of the house will break your heart into a thousand pieces.

'You may cry the day you discover your first gray hair or when your aging body no longer responds to your commands. Then, how you will long for the days of your youth.

'One day you may see sadness hidden behind your husband's eyes and you'll think he may be wondering if he made all the correct life choices. You might begin to doubt your importance to him, and those doubts will make you sad. The two of you will disagree, sometimes bitterly, and you'll want to lash out at the man who stole the girl from within you. But you won't. You will go into the bedroom, close the door and cry into this handkerchief instead.

'Conversely, there will be days when you're sick as a dog and can barely hold your head up. He will open a can of chicken noodle soup; bring a steaming bowl of it to you on a tray along with a beautiful rose from your own garden. You'll surely need this handkerchief on those days to hold the tears of love for the man you married.

'This piece of cloth, this handkerchief, has been washed in the tears of our family's women for such a long time. Mine, my mother's, her mother's before her. We have all used it to hold at least some of our sadness. Keep it close to you, daughter. Someday the past may help you to find whatever it is that you are searching for.'

The writing continued in Babe's mother's own hand.

"I leave you now, dear daughter-in-law I never knew, with the hope that you'll discover all of the things I so wanted to show you myself. It is my legacy to you and to your children."

It was signed, "Dolly."

I sat cross-legged on the attic floor under a naked light bulb for a long while and cried. I cried for not ever having known such a remarkable woman. Then I gently unpinned the handkerchief from the box and wiped away my tears.

THE GRANDKIDS FROM HELL

"Our grandchildren accept us for ourselves, without rebuke or effort to change us, as no one in our entire lives has ever done, not our parents, siblings, spouses, friends— and hardly ever our own grown children."—Ruth Goode

HAIL BLOODY MARY

"It's Not Just for Breakfast Anymore!"

"I want pancakes!"

"I want a fried egg sammich!"

"Make mine waffles!"

A cacophony of breakfast commands bounces off the sides of the stove. My head is spinning like an RCA Victor turntable, circa 1945.

It is seven o'clock in the morning and I don't even speak English before eight. Even then, Babe safely communicates with me by speaking only in one-syllable words.

With that in mind, somebody needs to tell me how to decipher the constant flow of food orders spewing from the mouths of the Grandkids from Hell.

Tightening my grip on the kitchen counter top (my lifeline to the real world), I take a deep breath and shout, "Hold it! I can only hear one person at a time. Now, two of you hush and one of you speak."

"I want pancakes!"

"I want a fried egg sammich!"

"I want waffles!"

"French Toast!"

"Fried chicken!"

"Mac and cheese!"

The walls begin to close in on me as the demands of three pint-sized versions of their daddy reach the sound level of a 747 taking off in the next room. The clock on the wall says seven-oh-nine. Is there no way I might justify a martini at this hour? No? How about a Bloody? It's tempting.

"Listen up, kids. I'll do my best to accommodate your requests, but you have to speak softly. Very, very softly. One—at—a—time."

The room is immediately filled with silence as the three sets of gaping eyes roll heavenward in unison. Big sighs all around as though they have been preparing all of their lives for this very moment.

"Now then, that's much better. I'll point to one of you and you will then tell me what you want for breakfast. Then I'll point to the next one and then the next. Keep in mind, fellas, that I am not Julia Child and this is not a short-order kitchen. Got that?"

They blink in sync.

"Who's Julie's child? Is she kin to us?"

"Forget Julia. I am not nor have I ever been Miss Betty Crocker, either. There. I know you know who Betty is."

They give each other a blank look then cock their heads in my direction.

"Is she the one you mean when you say 'one more martini' and I might have to check in to 'The Betty'?"

"No, but it's a thought and a darn good one. You guys are making me want to eat a bottle of aspirin before my first cup of Starbucks. One more time…Martha Stewart. Everybody knows her!"

"Martha went to jail, Mammy."

Whoa! I have new respect for Burns, the middle child who is normally soft-spoken and quieter than the other two. He watches CNN. Up to this moment, I thought the only thing he absorbed from daytime TV was Spongebob Squarepants.

"Well, I think ol' Martha passed GO and received a GET OUT OF JAIL FREE pass, boys. She a resourceful and creative woman, you know. That said, I still don't want to emulate her. Now, once again, what do you want for breakfast?"

"What's a M-you-late?"

"Nevermind! Just tell me what you want to eat, please. It's the crack of dawn and my migraine will not allow me to conjugate verbs at this hour. What do you want to eat, Burns?"

He closes his eyes and rolls his head back. "I'm thinking," he says, "that I would very much enjoy blueberry pancakes with a dollop of whipped cream and some of those little chocolate twirly things on top. You know what I mean, Mammy. Emeril uses them to decorate his cakes."

"Uh huh, and I'd like a new Jaguar. Get real, kid."

He clams up and starts thinking again.

I skip to Parker, the youngest, the one who normally wants his meals done up in chocolate. "How about you, sweetie pie. What can Mammy fix for you this morning?"

"Franco American Ravioli, please."

Whoa! We must have gone through a time warp while I was busy blinking. Is it suppertime so soon? I gaze at my watch. *Dream on, girl.*

"Parker, we don't do ravioli before the sun is over the yard arm, dear. Think buttery white grits and scrambled eggs with a dollop of yummy cheese on top, okay?"

"Yuk."

I go to my oldest grandson. "Okay, Bugs. What say you? Do you have a taste for something especially breakfasty this morning?"

He clears his throat. "Yes ma'am, I do. I would like to start with a Mimosa. Freshly squeezed orange juice in a chilled stemmed glass, if you please, Mammy. Then, perhaps Eggs Benedict with slices of fresh mango or papaya on the side, sprinkled with slivered almonds. Uh huh. I think that will do nicely."

He watches as I pour Mr. & Mrs. T into a glass and add liberal amounts of Stolchinaya to it.

"Or, Mammy, if a Mimosa is too over the top, I'll settle for a Bloody."

Using my free hand (the one not tilting the Bloody to my lips) I yank open the pantry door and grab a box of Cheerios. I stick a couple of bananas under my chin, then plop everything down on the kitchen table. I drag three cereal bowls and three spoons from the cupboard and set them down in front of my delightful Grandkids from Hell.

I take a long sip of my Bloody Mary, and smile as lovingly as such an early hour will allow me. "If anybody in this room gets to drink a Bloody, it dang well better be me. It's pip, pip and cheerios to you. If you need me for anything else, just phone "The Betty.""

FAMILY FEUDAL DE-DEE

"I hate turkeys. There's turkey ham, turkey bologna, turkey pastrami.
Someone needs to tell the turkey: man, just be yourself."—Mitch Hedberg

Babe and I are driving to South Carolina to spend Thanksgiving Day with family. Well, my family. Babe would just as soon stay home with his eyes glued to the football games. I, on the other hand, cannot seem to pull *my* eyes away from the steering wheel where his knuckles turn whiter with each mile we take. He does this as if it will keep us from plunging, Captain Nemo style, to the bottom of the Atlantic Ocean. The fact that we are fifty miles away from any form of seawater doesn't faze him.

"Can't you lighten up a little bit, Babe? Everything will work out fine. You'll see."

He fires a look at me, followed with a long-winded sigh that all of the Barrymores, dead or alive, would envy. "Spending Thanksgiving with your EX-family is not my idea of how to lighten up." He says this through teeth clenched to the point of shattering.

My son, bless his pointed head, had the bright idea a few months back to get us all together—not to talk turkey—but to eat it. That translates to: Babe, me, my ex-husband and his new wife. My ninety-four year old ex-mother-in-law, long since gone beyond hard of hearing into total deafness, has also been invited. As sweet and nice as she is, talking turkey or anything else with her could win the challenge of the day prize.

The Grandkids from Hell will be there. All five of them. The last time I counted, the average turkey hopped around on two legs. ALL five grandkids have called dibs on that particular piece of the bird's anatomy, of course. I plan to sample enough wine prior to the meal so that any position I might take on the subject cannot be construed as relevant.

Babe, staring straight ahead, releases one hand from the steering wheel and pointedly flexes it back and forth in mid-air.

"Circulation bothering you, honey?"

He gives me another look just short of a dagger.

"What am I supposed to say to your ex-husband," he asks. "The only thing I know about the man is that we have absolutely nothing in common."

I roll my eyes and clear my throat. "Well, I wouldn't exactly say *that*."

"Oh! Right. I can see it now. Me and the Ex drinking Bloody Marys while discussing the finer points of being married to the same woman."

"I like that" I say, "especially the finer points part. That should take about two minutes. Just stick to sports, Babe. It's the universal language of men, right? You can't go wrong talking about football."

"Might as well *talk* about it since we won't be *watching* it like everybody else in the civilized world." He lets out a turbo sigh and I could swear it rattled the hood ornament on the car ahead of us.

We drive on in silence for another fifteen or so minutes with Babe trying to set a sighing out loud record of some sort. Like I am unaware of his displeasure? His irritation at having to give up the football game in order to leave the island in time to make the one o'clock dinner has not eluded me.

Hoping to start up a conversation centered on his second favorite subject (food), I say, "They ordered a ham from the Honey Baked place and also a smoked turkey. We certainly won't leave the table hungry, will we?"

Another turbo sigh. The car ahead of us swerves to the right. "Are you telling me that when we walk through your son's kitchen door, we will NOT smell plain, ordinary, bought at Winn-Dixie on special, twenty-odd pounds of Butterball turkey slowly roasting in the oven?"

"Yep. I'd say that about sums it up."

"And are you saying that we won't be bringing home thick slices of leftover white, UN-smoked turkey? The very one that desperately calls my name at midnight? The ordinary, un-smoked bird I look forward to sandwiching between two slices of white bread in the middle of the night after a Thanksgiving feast?"

"That pretty much covers it, Babe. Unless, that is, you get a sudden craving in the middle of the night for ham, in which case we might be able to arrange something."

He looks at his watch, and then peers at the mileage marker on the side of the road. I can almost hear his brain calculating the distance between where we are now and how long it would take us to get back home should he suddenly whip the car around. His eyes slowly stray to my side of the car where I sit poised, waiting for him to make his move. "Don't even think about it," I say, my eyes sending daggers at him.

He gives me the wide-eyed innocent look, the one normally reserved for those times when he doesn't want me to know how much he spent on a new putter or driver, then he clears his throat.

"I was merely thinking of all the starving people in the world who would be more than happy to have a turkey to eat today, smoked or otherwise."

"You were?" And I was thinking the worst. Now, this is the man I married, the most unselfish, loving, kind person I ever met. How could I ever have thought otherwise? I should have known better.

"Yep," he says as chalk whiteness slowly returns to his knuckles. His hands are fastened like leeches to the steering wheel. "How about we round up a few hungry homeless people and bring them with us. We'll drop 'em off at Skip's house then head for the nearest hospital. Hospitals always serve turkey on Thanksgiving and Christmas…the regular kind, the normal kind with gravy and mashed potatoes and cranberry sauce. I bet we could even buy some extra slices to take home. For later, you know?"

"Patients aren't allowed to make midnight runs to the hospital kitchen for turkey sandwiches, Babe. Think about that before you pick up any starving hitchhikers."

He gives me a sidelong glance, shakes his head and lets go with a big, last sigh before turning into Skip's driveway. "Ham is good," he says. "Ham sandwiches? Even better."

JOHN WAYNE BROWN: THE TALE OF THE MISFORTUNE COOKIE

"Old hippies don't die, they just lie low until the laughter stops and their time comes round again."—Author: Joseph Gallivan

I have managed to quasi-quiet the Grandkids from Hell by stuffing their faces with really bad Chinese food that cost more than an entire week's wages. Even the fortune cookies were absurd. Mine said, "Grass is green." Duh.

Praying for no MSG repercussions, I pile the boys into the car and drive around aimlessly while trying to think of a doable way to keep them from killing each other on my watch.

I get what I believe to be a bright idea. "Hey, y'all haven't read your fortune cookies yet. Let's hear 'em."

Burns, the number two kid, jumps right in. "Me first! It says, 'Beware of authority.' That means I should beware of you. Right, Mammy?"

I'm thunderstruck. Among other appellations, at one time or another, I have been labeled a Throwback to the Sixties, a protester of harmful things thrust upon an unsuspecting public, a rebel, a troublemaker, even. To label me as an authority figure is like calling Osama bin Laden a Peacenik.

"Do not go there, kiddo," I tell him. "Do not even think it." I suck air through my nose, blow it out through my mouth, and slowly the relaxation response kicks in.

"Okay! Who's next? Who wants to tell us what their secret fortune says." (I often use the word "secret" when I need to get them involved in something other than the eminent demise of one of their siblings.)

Parker shrugs his six-year-old shoulders and gives me his quirky grin that never fails to make me want to eat him up. "I do, Mammy. I wanna tell my secret fortune, but I can't read too good yet."

My number one grandchild, Bugs, yanks the quarter-inch sized paper written in six-point type, from his brother's hands and begins to read.

"'It's a dog eat dog world.' Duh! That belongs on a can of Alpo, if you ask me."

Parker is quick on the draw. "So who asked ya?"

I foresee the launching of a war not so civil, so I grab the instigator seated next to me in the passenger seat and squeeze his arm. Hard. No, it is NOT a pinch. "Why don't you take your turn now, sweetheart?"

"'Meet trouble head on,' it says." He wrinkles his nose. "Like a person can meet trouble with his head off?" He leans over towards me. "By the way, Mammy. Where are we going?"

I don't have a clue but as long as they're not braining each other, I plan to keep right on trucking down the highway.

"How about I take y'all to the place where your daddy lived when he was a little boy?" The silence in the car is deafening; they were hoping for Dairy Queen.

"We lived next to a power plant on the banks of the Edisto River. It was kinda cool because we could walk out our front door and go fishing anytime we wanted to."

It's been way over thirty years since I was anywhere near the place. Desolate back then, I can only imagine what it's like today. The entrance gate, surprisingly, is wide open as we approach, and there is not a soul in the guard shack. I sally forth with aplomb and boogie on down the macadam road that leads to the river.

I look all around me when I put on the brakes at the only stop sign around. "Mercy! Things sure do look different than they used to." Before continuing, I look left, then right, and see nothing alive and nothing moving. Except for the billowing smoke coming from the large chimneys, the place looks deserted. As we near the river's edge where our house once sat, I point to the spot where our beagle, Batman, became a full-course meal for a bad tempered, hungry alligator.

Rounding a slight bend in the road, I glance in the rear view mirror in time to see a truck sprinting up behind me with the headlights blinking in furious succession.

"Uh oh, boys. We got trouble in River City."

Parker pipes up with, "Mammy, you talk funny."

"Yeah, I know. You have to remember that I am a product of the sixties. We invented a whole new language."

I pull the car over near a ditch and wait for the two security guards to swagger towards us like a couple of John Wayne wannabees. Attempting to look tough, the big guy with the red neck and Army surplus helmet frowns menacingly while snapping open his gun holster.

I smile wider than I knew was possible while batting the dickens out of my baby blues. "Hi there! Is there a problem?"

"DIN'T YOU SEE THAT STOP SIGN BACK YUNDER?"

"Uh, huh. I saw it. I stopped. Wasn't that what I was supposed to do?"

"THIS HERE IS PRIVATE PROPERTY. WHAT BIDNESS YOU GOT HERE?"

I hadn't noticed a No Trespassing sign, but maybe I missed it. I quickly decide that I'd better try to talk my way out of whatever it was that I did wrong.

"Listen, I used to live out here years and years ago. These are my grandkids." I keep that Ipana smile on my face and point to the boys who are so still and quiet it scares me. "We drove out here so I could show them where their daddy learned how to fish for Edisto River catfish, and where Batman got eaten up by an alligator."

John Wayne One looks at John Wayne Two. They nod in sync.

"STEP OUT OF THE CAHR!"

Overcome by a surge of adolescent courage, Number Two Grandson from Hell starts beating on the window. "You better leave her alone, you big bully! She didn't do anything. Batman was a dog." That, of course, makes no more sense to them than when I said Batman got eaten by an alligator. No matter. I'm proud of the little tyke.

John Wayne One orders me out again and that's when what is left of my sixties attitude rises like a flakey buttermilk biscuit. Lifting my chin, I make eye contact with him, which is almost impossible since his eyes are nearly covered by the rusty helmet. "No. I will not get out of my car. Suppose you tell *me* who *you* are and with what authority you have stopped me. Give me your name, rank and serial number."

I am in big time Rebel Mode now and it feels so good. In the back seat, however, the three Grandkids from Hell are in what appears to be serious Mute Mode. Lizard lips are plastered over their faces and their eyes look like fried eggs, sunny side up. They haven't been this silent since their first Trimester. Hoping to transmit reassurance, I grin in their direction and give them the thumbs up. But the only thing they seem to notice are the two heavies standing by the car door with a death grip on their holstered guns.

John Wayne One frowns at me but I maintain my rebellious eye contact. "My name is Jason Brown and this here is Wayland Hambright. We're security." He stammers, I notice, when he asks to see my driver's license, which gives me confidence that I might yet win this round. (I readily admit that I may have been a tad haughty when I whipped my license out of my purse and thrust it under his nose.)

He takes one quick look. "THIS AIN'T A DRIVER'S LICENSE. IT'S A CREDIT CARD!" John Wayne Brown is yelling much too close to my face and I do not appreciate the fact that he ate chili and beans for lunch.

"Whoopsy," I say demurely and hand over the real McCoy. "Credit cards are like finger magnets to the ladies, you know." He doesn't even pretend to get my clever quip.

Number Three Grandkid from Hell hiccups, something he only does when he is nearly frozen with fear. The doctor claims it is far better than sucking his thumb.

I look over John Wayne Brown's shoulder and see the only house still standing on the property. It is dilapidated and looks ready to fall down with the next strong wind. I point to it. "There were six of these houses when we lived out here," I say in a forlorn voice.

The eyes on the Green Beret wannabee are slits. Clearly, he doesn't give a hoot. "Ain't nobody lived out here in thirty years or more."

"Ya think?" I retort and immediately regret it.

"This here's a power plant, lady. We got hired on to look out for turrorists 'cause we was once in the Guard. Theys turrorists all over the place, lady. Sneaky sons of…" He stops short and glances at the three boys in the back seat waiting for him to use the "B" word. "We don't cotton to people sneaking in here like you done today. You gotta have official bidness to get anywheres near this plant. Understand?"

I look at him strangely. "No, I don't understand. Why are you afraid of tourists?"

"TURRORISTS! TURRORISTS! Them what's gonna take over our country if we don't round 'em all up."

A loud hiccup bubbles out from the back seat.

"Terrorists? You think we look like *terrorists?*" I sneak a peek in the mirror. It's true, I need a haircut and my nails could certainly use some attention, but I don't look a thing like a terrorist. If I did, I'm sure Babe would have mentioned it.

"We're just doin' our job, ma'am. Protecting the good citizens from them that would do us harm."

I am about to retort, "And Brownie, you're doing a heck of a job." But when I glance again at the white-as-grits faces of my grandkids, I bite my tongue nearly in half and say nothing. No doubt my clever jab would fly right over ol' John Wayne Brown's head anyway.

"Since you ain't got no bidness here," he continued. "I speck you jist better turn that lil' foreign car of yours around and head on out the same way you come in. Fact is, we'll be happy to escort you out."

As we leave John Wayne One and John Wayne Two, I blow them both a kiss followed with a peace sign, which they cannot possibly comprehend. As soon as the open gate is far behind us, Burns pipes up with a decent imitation of an Elvis concert M.C.

"Attention ladies and gentlemen. The turrorists have done left the premises."

The Hills Are Alive

"If you come to a fork in the road, take it."—Yogi Berra

Babe and I have been looking forward to spending the entire month together in a cozy little cabin in a cozy little town nestled in the North Carolina Mountains. With one General Store, one cafe and a one-woman operated post office, our chosen place promises to be the perfect spot for a secluded, second honeymoon.

The town is set miles away from I-26 or anything even resembling a straight road to anywhere. We get lost three times before Babe grudgingly agrees to ask for directions from a toothless man standing on the side of the road. The fellow has tight lips that barely move when he speaks and beady eyes that glare at us with a great deal of suspicion.

"He probably thinks we're revenuers," I whisper to Babe.

We arrive at our cabin late in the afternoon and congratulate ourselves for having chosen a spot so remote that the Grandkids from Hell couldn't find with a NASA satellite tracking system.

"Let's check out that cute little restaurant I saw in town, Babe. Aren't you starving?"

At the Green Apple Cafe, we sit down next to the other two customers in the place. While we're waiting for service, Jesse, a middle-aged dude with deep wrinkles and a long, gray ponytail, is all too happy to entertain us with tall tales and local legends while strumming on a homemade Mountain Dulcimer. After a bit, Delores, who is the owner, server, cook and bottle washer appears at our table and yawns. Who can blame her?

"Tonight's special is mesquite broiled salmon, fresh asparagus, sliced local tomatoes and real mashed potatoes. It's $5.95."

Did she say $5.95? We gawk at each and wonder when it was we hopped on a time machine that catapulted us back to the Fifties. One look at the wine list and we were certain we had departed the Twentieth Century. But heck! After driving all day, the tart, slightly fruity bouquet in Ripple ain't half bad.

I look deeply into Babe's brown eyes. "Isn't this romantic? No crowds or traffic, no over-priced meals, no uppity tourists. It's turning me on, Babe."

The next morning, he drops me off at the General Store to shop for groceries while he drives off down the road, hell-bent on finding the closest golf course.

Inside the store, sawdust covers the floor and I spend the next few minutes dumping it out of my sandals. I look at items on the shelves that only my grandmother might remember and she went to her great reward over thirty years ago. Sour Gum Molasses, dusty bottles of black stove polish, wooden clothespins and Black Drought Laxatives.

I see a bin full of local tomatoes, corn and okra and force myself to stifle my euphoria. I'm so giddy, I could jump up and down and stack greasy b.b.'s. Gently squeezing the red, robust Better Boys, I salivate with thoughts of a BLT.

I am completely lost in my fantasy when Charley, the octogenarian owner of the store introduces himself. For the next Half hour he tells me more than I want to know about his spastic colon and erratic PSA count. I blush with every mention of his bodily fluids, but he is obviously blind to my discomfort. Suddenly, he switches subjects and before I can catch up to him, he is carrying on about his sister Agnes.

"Ninety-three years old," declares Charley, "and she's mad as a wet hen 'cause the doctor done told her she couldn't go pick blackberries no more to make jelly which she loves to do."

"How come," I inquire, just to be polite. I'm wondering why Agnes, at her delicate age, doesn't buy herself some Smuckers and spend her remaining days watching reruns of "The Young and the Restless."

"Allergies," he tells me. "She cain't go up the hill without sneezing her fool head off. It jist wouldn't do at all for Agnes to sneeze herself into a coronary, now would it?"

Charley, being the only butcher within fifteen miles, provides fresh meat, fish and produce to the Green Apple Cafe next door. His cousin owns the cafe and is none other than Delores of last night's incredible salmon and asparagus for $5.95. A common door between the two buildings remains open during the day so that when somebody orders a hamburger, Delores can yell out, "Grind me off a pound, Charley!"

By the time Babe returns, I am up to date on all the latest gossip in this tiny community and can blurt out people's names and current ailments like I've known them all my life. Babe yawns as we make our way back up the hill to our cozy, romantic cabin, all ours for twenty-nine more days.

I squint my unbelieving eyes and stare out the window as we round the bend. "Hey, Babe. That looks like…Naaah, it can't be. Ohmygawd, it is!"

Babe cries, "How did they find us?"

The Grandkids from Hell are standing by the side of the road, waiting to pounce.

Babe starts shaking like he's got a new case of St. Vidas Dance. For a mere second, I consider throwing him to the wolves, whipping the car around and coasting silently back down the hill. But my grinning son interrupts any plan of retreat before it can be implemented. He is standing knee-deep amid the chaos and he's looking pretty much like a basset hound caught in quicksand.

"Hey, Mom! We thought we'd surprise you!"

I choke back the two questions I am itching to ask: *How did you find us and how long will you be staying?*

"I'm starving to death, Mammy!" Burns sidles up and gives me a cursory hug and kiss. "Whatcha' got to eat in those grocery bags?"

Bugs shoves him out of the way and starts to nag. "You just inhaled two hamburgers and a milk shake. Duh! You can't be hungry."

Burns fixes him with a look. "Just shut up. You don't know squat," to which Bugs tells *him* to shut up which launches the shut up yourself contest that's still going on to this day.

Parker pushes Bugs out of the way and crawls up the side of the car like a tree frog. I am so wishing I knew how to get back on that time machine.

"Mammy," the little tyke grabs me around the neck with sticky chocolate fingers and just hangs there, the rest of his forty pounds dangling and thumping on the side of my car. "Can I sleep in your bed with you tonight?"

I sneak a peek at Babe whose tears are now free-falling down his shell-shocked face. He's muttering, "Why me, God?"

The honeymoon, as they say, is officially over.

MARRIED WITH PETS

*"I never married because there was no need. I have three
pets at home that answer the same purpose as a husband.
I have a dog that growls every morning, a parrot that swears
all afternoon, and a cat that comes home late at night."*—Marie Corelli

The Neverending War Tale

"Dogs tend to bravado. They're braggarts.
In the great evolutionary drama, the dog is
Sergeant Bilko, the cat is Rambo."—James Gorman

Appropriately named Tallulah Blankhead, born north of the Mason-Dixon Line without a rebel bone in her overweight body, went AWOL yesterday. She's our dog and she has an intellect rivaled only by garden tools. She has never once left the back yard by herself. Why? Because she is obsessively attached to Babe, her food bowl and her favorite toy, a pale green stuffed rabbit appropriately named Mr. Babe.

At first, when I missed her, I thought she may have wandered onto the golf course and got boinked in the head by an errant Titleist. But when I scanned the course as far as my eye could see, I saw no sign of her at all. I didn't even see a range ball.

Twenty minutes later, I was wringing my hands like a parent with a daughter out on a first date. If Tallulah had not always been such a lily-livered pooch hovering alongside her over-protective keepers, I would not have been so concerned. It was totally out of character for her to go astray. Maybe she *was* out on a first date.

When calling and calling her produced no better results, I shut up and listened for her incomparable Cockapoo woof. It took a few minutes, but I finally heard her barking and it sounded like she was miles away.

My immediate thought was that Tallulah Blankhead's obesity had somehow put her in peril, so I shifted into high maternal mode. I even thought of sprinting like a roadrunner to the gun rack and loading that sucker up with as many bullets as I could find. I'd have been packing heat to the rescue.

The truth is, I am a chicken when it comes to guns. Tallulah, bless her fat little heart, was not born with that lily liver of hers, she got it by osmosis from me. Instead of snatching an assault weapon, I grabbed the car keys. My mission? To rescue Babe's precious, dumber than a box of hair, dog.

Two blocks away, I spied our Humvee lookalike dog. She was snarling at a fire hydrant that some Southern patriots had painted gray and white to resemble a corpulent Confederate soldier. Yankee dog Tallulah Blankhead, feeling a call to arms, had woofed herself into a war whoop.

I practically sat on the horn. "Tallulah Blankhead," I yelled. Abruptly, she tore her eyes away from Robert E. Lee long enough to glance in my direction, puff up her chest, then tear into General Lee as if he were drenched in Eau de Alpo.

"Hush your mouth, dawg, and get your fat ass in this car," I yelled again, in what I thought to be my most material voice. When she ignored me, I jumped out of the car, yanked her by the scruff of the neck and dragged her fat, fluffy fanny into the back seat. To her credit, she had the good grace to hang her head and look sheepish.

On the way back home, I asked myself what could have caused her to stray from her obsessively natural habitat. Why had Babe's cowardly Cockapoo left the familiarity of hearth and home to desert her post, only to get waylaid by a fire hydrant dressed to kill in Rebel Grey? Had the recently introduced meals for over the hill, over-indulged, overweight canines, not measured up to her epicurean palate? What, I wondered, made Tallulah Blankhead go AWOL?

There are none so blind as those who will not see. The answer was in front of me.

Sophie Sorrowful, a stray white kitten rescued from the clutches of the grim reaper, had to be the reason. In only two weeks time, she had managed to launch a coup d'état that rivaled anything ever cooked up in a Banana Republic. Lord only knows what kind of propaganda she had been meowing in order to spark the obvious rebellion. Armed with outrageously large blue eyes and saber sharp teeth and nails, she came, she saw, she conquered. Almost overnight, Sophie Sorrowful snatched the throne away from Tallulah the Tank Blankhead to promptly proclaim herself the Queen of Queens.

However, Tallulah Blankhead, unlike General Lee, decided *not* to surrender. Ever since her freshly infused resolve, gleaned while snarling at a fat fire hydrant, she is determined to stand her ground. For Overweight Tallulah Blankhead, that fire hydrant corner became her Fort Sumter. Armed with newfound strength, she constantly prepares to defend her position as Queen of the Hill.

On the other hand, if she thinks that Sophie Sorrowful's Appomattox is a'coming, she's got another think coming. This cat and dog war ain't gonna be over till it's over.

SITTING SHIVA FOR MISS FANCY

"The term Shiva is derived from a Hebrew word meaning "seven."
It refers to the seven-day period of mourning which takes place following a burial.
During this period of time, family members suspend all worldly activities, and devote
full attention to mourning the deceased. This is what is called "sitting Shiva."

"My husband says I might as well just cover my head in cellophane wrapping paper and tie it with a red ribbon," said Shelby Jo. "I'm inclined to agree with him."

"Personally," I told her, "as a fashion accessory, I seriously doubt you'll make the cover of 'W,' so how come you're thinking cellophane wrap?"

She batted her eyes and grinned. "He thinks I'm such a sucker when it comes to sick kittens that I might as well make myself look like a lollipop."

I couldn't argue with that kind of logic. It's as though Shelby Jo unconsciously transmits a signal from her house directly to every stray cat within a ten-mile radius. I'm told that some cats, like some kids, instinctively locate the best neighborhood hangout. Shelby Jo's house became a CAThedral with Shelby as the feline answer to Mother Teresa.

"What up with the lollipop thing, Shelby Jo?"

"It's a long, creepy story. Are you sure you want to hear it," she asked.

"I'm all ears."

"Some months back, a kitten with feline leukemia showed up at my back door. I knew right away the poor lil' thing wouldn't live very long, but what else could I do but take it in and try to make her last days on earth memorable."

(In order to have that kind of compassion, I suppose one would need to believe that a cat's memory storage rolls over into the afterlife, but I didn't mention it.)

"Did you give the poor lil' thing a name?"

"Oh, of course I did! She deserved at least that. I named her Miss Fancy, and it was perfect. She wasn't on earth for very long, but she made such a splash. Right away, Miss Fancy became the neighborhood starlet. She even had permanent "eyeliner" around her larger than normal eyes and a beauty mark on her nose."

Shelby Jo got teary at this point and had to stop and blow her nose.

"A few weeks ago, the inevitable happened." She blew her nose again and wiped her eyes. "Little Miss Fancy died and it seemed to me like she hadn't been with us long enough, so we buried her in the back yard and planted some impatiens at the site. I felt a little better after that."

The following week, Shelby Jo told me that she left town on a business trip. When she called home, she was told that the next door cat named O.K., along with Shelby Jo's other cat Bailey, were sitting on top of Miss Fancy's grave! They had been parked there for several hours! As it turned out, the two cats sat Shiva with Miss Fancy on and off for seven straight days. Shelby Jo's son, an avid photographer, had it documented on five rolls of film, just in case he needed to prove to his parents that he was not on Hallucinogenic drugs.

Later that week, I discussed this phenomenon with St. Simon's cat Veterinarian, Dr. Lisa. I told her the tale Shelby Jo told me about the two cats sitting Shiva on Miss Fancy's grave. I was curious to find out whether or not that kind of cat behavior is considered normal.

Dr. Lisa told me that she had often heard stories about cats visiting graves. She offered the medical explanation that cats can continue to give off oxygen even after they are dead and buried. Then she told me that evidence is being gathered regarding feline sensory perceptions, and that the data is being seriously considered. (I didn't ask by whom.) Research, she added, is finding that cats are so sensitive that they are often lured toward other sick, dying or dead animals. They may even be drawn to sick children.

With Halloween right around the corner, I couldn't help but wonder if this type of graveyard behavior is how black cats got themselves paired up with broomstick witches, ghosts and goblins.

Although Shelby Jo still mourns for Miss Fancy, she told the Doodah Sisters last week at lunch that yet another under the weather kitten showed up at her back door shortly after Miss Fancy had left the building, so to speak. Sick with an upper respiratory infection and way too thin, Shelby Jo named her, appropriately, Twiggy.

The kitten could barely breathe because of the congestion, and her sense of smell was blocked completely. She had little or no appetite, so Shelby Jo had to teach her how to eat. That, of course, was before Dr. Lisa waved her magic antibiotic wand.

Now Twiggy goes around sniffing and smelling everything in site. A whole new world has opened up for her, thanks to Shelby Jo and Dr. Lisa.

"I may have to rename her soon because she's about to eat me out of house and home!" Shelby Jo gave out this new information with a big, fat grin on her face. She is obviously in love with Miss Twiggy.

"What does the kitten look like," Mary Grace asked.

"She has black, mink-like hair, with some white on her face. Much like the other Twiggy, she is quite naturally the fashion plate. Get this: she wears white gloves on her paws with scallops around each and every pad. She also wears a white slip with a pilgrim collar."

"If you ask me," I said to Shelby Jo, "Twiggy's basic wardrobe has a far better chance of making it into 'W' than that idea you had of wrapping your head up in cellophane."

"No doubt about it," she replied. "Like they always say, we have a lot to learn from our animals. Who would have thought that would include the latest fashion trends."

POUND BYTES

"If you wish the dog to follow you, feed him."—*Unknown*

As he pours dry dog food into Overweight Tallulah Blankhead's bowl, Babe says, "Aw, she's not as fat as all *that*! She deserves to eat tasty food. Don't forget, she's a middle-aged female with a middle-age middle."

I roll my eyes. "If her middle gets any rounder we can slap a saddle on her and sell your gas guzzling SUV."

Tallulah the Tank sniffs at her one-half cup of low-calorie food designed for dogs with dietary needs. She looks up at me and I *know* I can read her thoughts: *You don't honestly believe I am going to eat this swollen birdseed, do you?* She sighs out loud. Ignoring the brown Eukanuba pellets, she plops her Butterball body down on the floor. VAROOOOOM! It sounds like a starting race at Daytona.

"Awww, poor baby," croons Babe. He spoons gravy, leftover from last night's country fried steak, into her bowl and begins to swish it around with his finger. "You can worry about dieting tomorrow, Tallulah Belle." (My Yankee husband was doing another bad imitation of Scarlett O'Hara.)

I stomp out of the room. "Why don't you buy her a mega bucket of KFC while you're at it, Babe? And don't forget the 'Nana Puddin'!"

He yells back, "She doesn't like bananas!"

Fat dogs run in the family. Well, Tallulah the Tank hasn't actually *run* anywhere since we had her spayed a few months after she was born. At this point in her life, walking from her bed to her bowl has become a major challenge. Jumping (as in up on the sofa) is completely out of the question, but I'm not complaining.

This eating frenzy all started with Winston, the Pug from Hell, who belongs to Babe's daughter. Built like Pac Man, Winston qualifies for the Eat Till You Pop Poster Dog.

"Why do you feed him so much, Laura," I ask while eying the two-foot tall eating machine supported on Popsicle stick legs.

"I used to give him the stuff you feed Tallulah, but it got too expensive."

"What, the dry food?"

"No, the emergency Vet. You see, when Winston gets hungry, he eats anything in sight. It's as though he's got an out of control eating disorder."

I look at Winston. "I can believe it. But, what's the emergency Vet got to do with it?"

She sighs. "Winston eats pantyhose. He has a passion for them."

"Get out!"

"It's true. Four times the vet had to extract a pair of my pantyhose from his uh…rectum. Now I make sure that he gets filled up on food instead of nylon."

She gazes lovingly at the breathing impaired Pug. "Is Mommy's baby still hungwy? Is the baby weddy for dessert?"

Offering Winston dessert goes way beyond overkill, but I'm wearing my only pair of pantyhose so I see no reason in the world to tempt that poor animal.

Our fat little Cockapoo has been sitting at my feet taking it all in. Every word. Winston aka Pac Man, is the teacher. Tallulah Blankhead is the student.

Laura happily prepares a butterscotch sundae, pops a cherry on top and then puts it on a linen placemat in front of her dog.

She sings, "My Winston is a happy Pug. He's my wit-tle lovey bug," while Pac Man Dog throws his head back and howls to high heaven. It is almost as bad as being trapped in an elevator with Kenny G.

I grab Tallulah the Tank with the intention of covering her eyes to the sundae, or at the very least, closing her ears to the duet. Busy inhaling leftover greasy smells from Winston's bowl of fried chicken livers and hash brown potatoes, Tallulah whips around and snarls at me. She bares her teeth and turns into Kujo. I can read her thoughts: *Touch me again, Mother Trucker and you'll be trucking to Bakersfield with one less wheel.*

I need to get her out of the room before she gets a longer look at the Pug from Hell slurping up that sundae. She has locked her legs so tight, however, that I need a cattle prod to move her. Glaring at me as I drag her into the living room, I'm even more positive I can read her thoughts: *I hate you! I don't want you to be my mommy any more. I want Laura to adopt me!*

For three days, our sulking dog does not eat one bite of her vitamin balanced, nutritionally enriched Eukanuba. Then suddenly the hunger strike is over and she stops pouting. Remarkably, I am again back in her good graces. She even licks my hand.

"What's with The Tootah," I ask Babe. "Did Winston eat her adoption papers or what?"

Babe stutters and sputters before finally blurting out the truth. "I told Laura to feed Tallulah some Winston food."

"You did not."

"Did, too. She was looking way too much like the dog from Auschwitz."

That was last Christmas and since that time, Tallulah is twice the dog we have always known and loved. Literally.

Babe hollers to me from the kitchen like a hillbilly. "Hey, Cap! I've figured out how we can make Tallulah Blankhead skinny again!"

I ease into the room. "And while you were being such a genius, did you also come up with a cure for the common cold?"

"Very funny."

I smile brightly. "Okay, then. How do you think we should whittle the weight off our little oinker?"

"Let's put her on the Atkins Diet."

I shake my head. "Sounds like you're running low on brain cells again, Babe. Time to plug in your charger."

He shrugs. "Listen up. Dogs are carnivores—natural meat eaters, right? If Dr. Atkins wasn't dead, he'd tell us in a heartbeat to put her on his diet."

I roll my eyes at him before examining the tiny bag of diet dog pellets I'd bought available only through a veterinarian at a hefty price. A quick mental calculation tells me I can buy filet mignon for a whole lot less and come home with change in my pocket.

"Babe, your on-again/off-again genius overwhelms me at times. I say we drive that gas guzzling SUV of yours to the store and buy our pudgy little pooch a big, fat T-bone."

He grins and winks those big brown Basset eyes at me. "Yeah, well maybe just a pound of ground round."

Pulling Her Own Strings

"If a cat could speak, it would say things like,
Hey, I don't see the problem here."—Roy Blount, Jr.

About three o'clock this morning Babe and I were awakened by a loud bumping and scraping sound coming from the family room. I heard it first and it like to scared me to death.

"Babe!" I shook him awake. "Get the baseball bat. We've got an intruder!"

"Go back to sleep. You're just having a bad dream." He rolled over and muttered, "I was having a really good one till you woke me up."

I shook him again.

"Oh, all right." Grumbling as he slid out of bed, he switched on the light and nearly blinded me. When the noise started up again, he stopped to listen, questioning the wisdom of facing an intruder while wearing polka dot boxers and brandishing a kid's baseball bat.

"Go!" I whispered a yell. "If it was Charles Manson, he would already be writing names on the walls with our blood."

He flicked on the den light to search the area, but the only thing he saw was the rear end of Sophie Sorrowful as she darted under the sofa. Rightly figuring that the cat was somehow responsible for the noise, he reached under the sofa to pull her out.

When Babe's hand began to probe around in her hiding place, Sophie Sorrowful darted out the other side and began a frenzied promenade around the room.

Dragging and bouncing my grandson Parker's forgotten yo-yo over the tile floor, she unwittingly repeated the sound that had awakened us.

It was a small yo-yo, not much larger than a fifty-cents piece. Parker had won it as a prize at Dave & Busters Arcade Casino in Jacksonville. Such an important prize that he forgot to take it home with him.

Bump, bump, bummmmmmp!

Babe gave chase and finally grabbed Sophie Sorrowful by the scruff of her neck. (He is convinced that she loves it when he does this, that she likens it to her mother picking her up when she was a kitten.) Holding her close to his sleep-encrusted eyes, he noticed for the first time that she had swallowed all but about three inches of the yo-yo string.

His first thought was to cut off the wooden part of the yo-yo with scissors, which would allow Sophie Sorrowful to swallow all of the string and eventually poop it back out. After only a nanosecond, however, he had a second thought, thank goodness. After all, it was a long string and well, it could take days, maybe weeks before the end of that string ever saw daylight. He decided to tug on it very gently.

"EEEEOOOOOWWWWWWOOOOOOOOOEEEEE!" shrieked Sophie Sorrowful.

Holding her as firmly as one can hold a squirming, screaming, frightened-out-of-her-mind cat with one hand, Babe yanked again on the string. Harder.

Sophie Sorrowful let out another, "EEEOOOOWWWOOOOOEEEEE!" which set off the burglar alarm and got me hopping out of my warm bed faster than a speeding bullet. I dashed into the den and saw Babe, clad in those silly polka dot boxers, standing stupidly in the middle of the floor. He was dangling a yukky looking yo-yo with two fingers while both he and Sophie Sorrowful took turns gagging.

Intuiting, as cats will do, that she had been delivered from a strange and eerie fate, Sophie Sorrowful now considers Babe to be her Don Quixote, her savior, her real life hero. The Man. She follows him around all day long, skillfully dodging his Size Eleven shoes with every step he attempts to take.

The fate of the yo-yo? Much like Jonah who was swallowed by the proverbial whale, that hard-won, impossible to digest yo-yo is history.

SOUTHERN FRIED, BOILED AND BAKED

"Any Southerner worth his piecrust knows that White Lily is the only flour worth stocking in the larder."

—Richard David Story, *New York magazine*

Good Ol' Southern Cookin'

True grits, more grits, fish, grits, and collards.
Life is good where grits are swallered.—Roy Blount, Jr.

Move over, Georgia peanut growers and make room for the South Carolina Peanut Gallery.

Last year Georgia's good neighbors to the North were polled by Charleston's *Post and Courier* Food Editor in order to ascertain South Carolina's most popular food. The ugly, no-color, lowly, salty, boiled peanut came out on top. Who'd have thunk it?

I was born and raised in South Carolina, but nobody polled me. If they had of, I might have jumped up and down cheering and hooraying for the good old bald peanut, as we Palmetto Staters like to call it. I love boiled peanuts and cannot, for the life of me, figure out why so many Yankees do not. On the other hand, my Yankee husband Babe considers them a gourmet delicacy. Go figure.

The plethora of All-You-Can-Eat Buffet restaurants up and down the East Coast is glaring evidence that we Southerners do enjoy our food. We're "good eaters," as Mama would say. Not only that, we are proud of our ability to take a garden-variety food, like the tomato, and literally cause it to do the Boogie Woogie in our mouths. Give me some white bread and Dukes Mayonnaise and I'll dance to that tune any old day of the week.

After reading the aforementioned food poll in the Charleston newspaper, I began to consider why it is that Southern cooking is so appealing, so memorable that Yankees go back up Nawth and try to duplicate it. They never do, of course, but it doesn't have a thing in the world to do with the ingredients. They were simply not born with the knack. You gotta have the knack.

Take your basic fried chicken dinners, for instance. Many people have forgotten what authentic fried chicken ever tasted like. We can thank Colonel Sanders for that. In his quest to be crowned Chicken King of the World, he concocted a gawd-awful seasoning that he poured over the unsuspecting fowl. Then he put the chicken *in the oven* and baked it! Yes ma'am, I said he baked it. To add insult to injury, he had the audacity to call it Kentucky *Fried*, and everybody gobbled it up. I don't believe for a minute that Kentuckians subscribe to the idea that baked chicken is the same as fried chicken, but KFC certainly did take them off the Kit Carson circuit.

You simply can't fry chicken in an oven. That bird has to be soaked in milk, eggs, salt and pepper. It absolutely *must* be thrown in a brown paper bag full of flour, and then fried in a crowded black iron frying pan full of Crisco and bacon drippings.

While that chicken is cooking, a big macaroni pie has to occupy a decent place in the oven. I want to make something clear: Macaroni Pie is *not* the same thing as Mac and Cheese, which Yankees like to eat as an entrée with a salad and French Bread on the side. They call that an entire meal. We don't do that down here.

Macaroni Pie means elbow macaroni baked with eggs, milk and lots of sharp, artery-clogging cheese and butter. In a Southern kitchen, the Macaroni Pie is already bubbling in the oven before that old yard bird makes it out of the brown paper bag.

Once those two things are done, a plate full of sliced tomatoes is generally passed around to everybody at the table; tomatoes picked that same morning from somebody's personal garden. Naturally, a jar of Dukes Mayonnaise is passed around with the tomatoes. Vidalia Onions and sliced cucumbers that are virtually drowning in vinegar complete this very Southern fried chicken meal. Almost.

Add to that, a steamer full of rice, green vegetables like Butter Beans, Kentucky Wonders or Collard Greens cooked in fatback or side meat. Now, those are the things that put the final touches to a fine Southern Sunday dinner.

A meal like that doesn't need biscuits. It doesn't need cornbread or mashed potatoes and gravy. It doesn't need one other thing except maybe a bowl of peach cobbler topped with home-churned ice cream.

We Southerners eat food like this and often live to be way up in our nineties. And why do you suppose that is? Maybe it's because in-between our summer meals, there is always a batch of boiled peanuts to munch on. Then there's Clemson Bleu Cheese and Ritz Crackers, ice-cold watermelon right out of the patch, Benne Wafers and 'Nana Puddin.' We *have* to live a long time so we can get around to eating it all.

How Do You Pronounce It?

"Without the chicken, boiled rice is just plain boring."—*Zola Sorrells Hall*

There was one particular meal in my mother's stable of menus that she fixed for our Sunday night suppers. Chicken Perlow. She served it with a tomato and lettuce salad dressed in Dukes Mayonnaise, and Sunbeam Brown 'n Serve rolls slathered in real butter. Occasionally, she would fix Spaghetti, the best in the world because our mother made it. Doesn't *everybody's* mother make *the* best spaghetti? But that's another story. This one is about Chicken Perlow, the Sunday night supper that I remember like it was yesterday.

The name Perlow is a Southern variation of the word Pilau or Pilaf. I don't know whether it was handed down from the days of slavery or what, but I suspect that the Africans who were brought to the South learned English as best they could. Since many of the white people already living here were often ignorant, certain words took on a pronunciation entirely different from the original. This was particularly true in the Lowcountry where many African dialects merged into one and became known as Gullah, a rhythmic dialect still spoken today along the coasts of South Carolina and Georgia.

Chicken Perlow was my all-time favorite comfort food, and still is. Several months after my mother died, I woke up with an enormous craving for it. Only then did I realize I had never once cooked it myself. Mama always prepared it. To make matters even worse, she died without ever giving me her recipe.

I broke down, started crying and thought I would never stop. I expect the tears were about much more than the Chicken Perlow, so when I finally straightened up I realized that I could call Aunt Polly. Surely she would have Mama's recipe since they cooked very much alike and shared recipes all the time. I was right. We both sniveled while I explained my plight.

"Honey, I don't have that recipe written down anywhere," she said.

My heart sank. I was so sure…

"But don't you fret, Sugah. I know it by heart and it's the easiest thing in the world to fix. Now here's what you do. Go get yourself a nice size cut-up fryer. (You could get a stewing hen but then you'd have to cut it up and that's just too much trouble.) You'll need two or three big stalks of celery diced up real nice, and two big ol' onions, cut up just like the celery. Two cans of chicken broth and enough water to cover everything up and a little bit of salt and pepper.

"Put it all in a big ol' pot and cook it till that chicken falls off the bone. Then take your chicken out and set it down on a plate so it can cool. After it gets so you can handle it, you want to take all the skin and bones off that ol' bird and set it aside.

"Now, here's what you need to do with the pot likker left from when you were stewing the chicken. You put it in the Frigidaire till all the fat rises to the top, and then you take a big spoon and get rid of it before you cook your rice. I don't want you clogging up your arteries like I did.

"The rest of the recipe is easy as pie. It's two cups of long grain rice, four cups of the pot likker (you might need to add a little bit of water to it), a Half a teaspoon of salt, a right good bit of black pepper, and two or three hard-boiled eggs, grated up on the fine side of your hand grater.

"Be sure you cook up your rice in the pot likker that still has all your celery and onions in it. You might have to add some water, but that's a matter of taste. Some people like their Perlow to be like a bog, but personally I never cared for it like that and neither did your mama. But if you want to, you can add a little bit more water to make your rice wetter and stickier.

"Now, after the rice is all done, at least 20 or 30 minutes, well then, you take your chicken and tear it all up into little pieces and mix it with your rice. That's when you want to taste it to see how much salt and pepper to add, if any. After you get all of that straight, you grate up those two boiled eggs and sprinkle them on top of everything.

"The real secret of Perlow is to serve it straight from the pot, Sugah. That way, it won't get cold on you, and you can keep going back for seconds as many times as you want to. Now. Ittn't that simple?"

TASTES JUST LIKE CHICKEN

"Heart Attacks…God's revenge for eating His animal friends."—anonymous

Billie Gail sighs contentedly. "I do believe I've died and gone to heaven. Nothing has ever tasted this good and you have got to have some. Lord knows there's a gracious plenty here. Just take one bite."

My stomach flips over for the thirtieth time as I gaze down at my plate full of an animal swimming around in onion gravy. Why didn't I become a vegetarian when I had the chance?

"Billie Gail, I gotta be honest, honey. I have lived in this world a long, long time without ever having eaten possum and it would be a shame to mess up my record. I don't mean to be rude, but I would have a real hard time chewing up and swallowing this little critter."

She grins. "Well, he might be a wee little bit tough, that's true. But he tastes just like chicken!"

I put down my fork. "Now why did you have to give him a gender, for god's sake? Next thing I know you'll be naming him. 'Hey, have a bite of Percival,' you might say."

Billie Gail stops trying to cut him with her recently sharpened utility knife. "Percival," she says. "I like it. I can nickname him Percy." She picks him up with her bare hands and groans with epicurean delight as she sinks her teeth into what looks like the critter's little arm.

I clear my throat in hopes of settling my stomach, although I seriously doubt anything short of major surgery will have any effect. "Aren't possums mammals? It doesn't seem to me that God meant for us to eat things that have pouches, B.G. Think about it! They carry their babies around in those pouches."

She stops chewing for a nano-second and looks me in the eye. *What a blonde thing to say,* she's probably thinking. With her mouth full of Percy she quickly contradicts me. "Nuh-uh. Not mammals. Marshupialz."

"Marshupialz? You mean Marsupials, right?"

Her mouth is so full that she abandons any effort to form words I might understand and simply nods her head.

"Good heavens! Like in kangaroo? With real *big* pouches?"

I'm wondering how long she will need to chew that bite of Percy before her jaws completely give out. It's beginning to annoy me when she attempts to speak again. "You're kinda obshessing on the pouch thang, aren't 'chu, girlfriend?"

I've never been a picky eater. A large portion of my life was spent in the South Carolina Low Country where wild things like catfish, quail, doves and deer were what we ate. Edisto River catfish is a delicate taste like no other. Farm raised? Get serious.

One time my brother and two of his friends ran over an alligator when gators were still on the endangered list. The boys jumped out to look at the "kill," and not knowing what else to do, they cut off its tail with a Swiss Army knife and brought it home to my mama. She segued right into Julia Child mode, chopped the tail into bite-sized pieces, then fried it like shrimp. Everybody agreed it was delicious. Even me! And guess what? It tasted just like chicken!

Billie Gail finally swallows that wad of marsupial named Percy, takes a deep breath and lets it out slowly, as if in relief. "I swear to my soul, girlfriend, you just gotta eat at least a little bit of this meat. You don't know what you're missing."

"I'll take your word for it Billie Gail." I pick up a napkin, reach across the table and wipe off little bits of leftover Percy from her chin.

"Dang straight. I know good food like a wino knows wine."

I realize how dumb that sounds, but I nod as though an image of Ripple did NOT immediately pop into my head.

"And you know what else? It really *does* taste just like…"

"DON'T GO THERE!"

"But it does. I'm telling you that this possum is every bit as good as…"

Dreading her next word, I close my eyes and pray for sudden, but temporary, deafness.

"…rattlesnake. Yum—mee."

I bolt from the table, knock over a chair and stumble over a footstool. Somehow, I make it to the bathroom just in time.

NO SHOES, NO SERVICE

"Guests, like fish, begin to smell after three days."—Benjamin Franklin

I am not a morning person. That is why when a girlfriend from my very distant past called to say that she would be stopping by "for a while early on Friday," the first words to leave my lips were, "How early is early?"

"Not a minute past eight o'clock," she responded.

I gulped back the impulse to say, "Sorry, wrong number." Instead, I sighed sincerely into the phone as though I was truly disappointed. "Oh, I'm so sorry. The thing is, we've already made plans for Friday night. I wish you'd have called sooner. Well, maybe next time you're in the area."

She giggled. "No problemo! I meant I would be there early on Friday *morning*."

My mind did a whirligig thing while I taxed my brain and tried to figure out why in God's name she was traveling at such a ridiculous time of day, and why she was planning to take a pit stop at my house before I'd had my first cup of Starbucks.

What kind of person comes to visit before eight a.m.? What kind of mind even thinks up such a plan?

"Oh, I get it," I offered. "You're staying overnight in Brunswick, right?" That was the only reasonable explanation I could think of.

"Oh, lord no," she said. "We're leaving Miami at 2 a.m."

In less time than it takes to blink, my lips parted wider than the Red Sea. "Did you say 'WE'?"

"Oh! Didn't I mention my daughter, her husband and their precious baby? We're all traveling together. It was my idea to start out on the trip after precious baby's bedtime so she wouldn't be so cranky."

My house was squeaky clean for the first time since we moved in three years ago. The furniture was shining with way too many coats of Pledge. The floors had been waxed and buffed to a fair-thee-well and I could actually see myself again in the mirrors, which was *not* going to be the most exciting part of my day.

The point of my obsessive cleaning had to do with a large cocktail party Babe and I were throwing the following night. I'd worked my tail feathers to the bone getting the house ready and I didn't want company coming in to mess things up.

"You'll be stopping somewhere for breakfast then," I said to her, hoping the no-frills service at this bus stop would delay their ETA.

"Would it be okay if we just grab a bite at *your* house. We don't want to wake up precious baby until we're ready to stop for a while. You understand, don't you?"

I did not understand. Why me? What did I ever do to deserve uninvited guests at such an ungodly hour of the day? Whatever I did, God, I'm sorry. I promise not to do it again!

They came anyway, and they were all barefooted. They messed up my kitchen. Fischer-Price was scattered all over my living room. They rested for far too long in my beds with fresh linens on it. When they did go, they left dirty dishes, dirty linens and dirty floors that needed a lot more than a broom. God willing, they would never be back.

NOT!

The phone rings. "If we might impose on you just once more…"

Hey God! Didn't you hear me when I said I was sorry?

"We'd be so grateful," she pleads. "Mom tells everybody what a loving, caring, generous, sensitive soul you are."

Awww, geezlueeeze. Where does one go to mainline Prozac?

They unload their huge conversion van just after midnight and not long after our last cocktail party guests have left. In the morning when I stumble to the kitchen for caffeine, they are already seated at the table waiting for breakfast.

Precious Baby demands waffles while her mother murmurs, "Just two poached eggs, bacon and coffee for me." The husband says, "I guess you'll have to make another pot of coffee. I woke up early and helped myself. Starbucks, isn't it? That's tasty stuff. We only buy the kind with the blue line across it."

No coffee? No freaking coffee? Am I in the middle of a bad dream or what?

Babe saunters in and takes one look at my face before backing out of the room faster than a roadrunner on speed. Cowardly Tallulah Blankhead tucks her tail and whines her way out of the room right behind him.

I stare at the houseguests from hell with the devil's fire leaping out of my eyes. "You drank all my coffee? (Notice I am using two syllable words.) "Waffles? Poached eggs? Bacon? Does this look like the IHOP to you? Do I look like your mother? I don't DO breakfast. I do coffee!"

"Uh, sorry 'bout that," he offers lamely.

"Well, buddy, sorry just doesn't cut it. Not with me before my Starbucks. But as you said, it's all gone. Like you suggested, I will make another pot and I'll drink it. All of it. All by myself. Want to know why?"

They nod their collective heads while Precious Baby screams hers off for waffles.

"I'll tell you why. Because you're fixing to get your considerably inconsiderate butts out of my kitchen and into that gas guzzling freight train you call a van before I get real nasty. Once in that van, you're gonna find another place to order breakfast. I don't give a hoot where that is, but you will most definitely disappear from my life forEVER."

I am not proud of myself at times like this when my nice-nasty nature emerges. But then again, I'm a Southern woman married to a Yankee. It comes with the territory.

Not Good Enough to Eat!

Wandering the aisles of Winn-Dixie on a Thursday afternoon, I look up and there's my old friend, Ivy Lee Johnson. It's been a year since I ran into her in this same store.

"Well, shut my mouth and call me smarty! If it ain't Cappygirl."

I grin, in spite of feeling conspicuous and much too exposed. People are gawking. Ivy's voice level is tantamount to a Space Shuttle taking off in the next aisle.

"Ivy Lee, look at you. You've lost so much weight I hardly recognized you."

Her grin is wide enough for me to see the sockets in her gums, which at one time may have held wisdom teeth, but that's debatable.

"Uh huh. I sho' did loose a little bit of weight," she singsongs loud enough to be heard in the meat department in the back of the store. "Yep. Sho' did."

"Well, give it up, girlfriend. How many pounds did you lose?"

Ivy Lee looks all around us as if to make sure she has captured the attention of a wide audience. "One hundred and fourteen and a quarter pounds," she announces to one and all, her grin expanding to the size of a sixteen-wheeler. Put a motor on that mouth and she could set a new record for cross-country travel.

"Whoa!" I am impressed. The first time I met her I remember thinking she might have been shapely at some time in her life, but too many visits to Sonny's Barbeque Pit had re-positioned the digits on her dress size. Looking at her now, though, it's hard to believe she is the same person.

"So tell me the truth. Who are you? And what did you do with my friend Ivy Lee?"

The loud cackle that echoes throughout the store makes me wish I had opted not to be quite so clever.

"Cappygirl, you are a hoot. You wanna know how I lost all my fat and became the sex goddess I am today, right? You *really* want me to tell you?"

Ivy Lee has been married six times that I know of. She explained to me once that the state of Georgia would allow her to marry only once more. "For that reason," she confided that day, "I decided to get real picky." That was, of course, a couple of years ago. Lord knows what has happened since.

"Do I want to know? Why, certainly I want you to tell me how you lost the weight, Ivy. But skip the sex goddess part, okay? Babe's blood pressure is way too high as it is."

She cackles loudly while rooting around in her pocketbook. "It's in here some place. I'll find it. Just gimme a minute, hon."

I crane my neck in an attempt to glimpse inside the piece of Samsonite she calls a purse. "What are you looking for, Ivy?"

"The piece of paper I wrote down my diet on." (She pronounces diet as dite.) "Here we go. If it hadda been a snake, I'da had enough time to tame it."

She thrusts a well-worn, smudged index card at me, the large, nearly faded out words written in pencil.

"The Spit Diet?" I start to laugh. "This is a joke, right?"

She quits grinning. Her expression changes to one of sober sincerity.

"Most certainly NOT. Look at me." She twirls around in the middle of Aisle Three like a reincarnated Pavlova. "Do I look like a joke to you?"

I assure her that she does not look like a joke and that I meant no disrespect, that she, in fact, looks terrific. "But, Ivy Lee, the Spit Diet sounds so, uh, uh…"

"So crazy?"

I nod my head. "Well, yeah, it does. Kinda. Sorta. What exactly is it?"

She climbs off her high horse long enough to get right in my face. I back up a foot. "This diet is so easy I can't believe I thought it up all by myself. I'm gonna write me a book and I betcha it'll outsell that Atkins fellow calling hisself a doctor."

I nod my head and smile encouragingly. "It says here you can eat anything you want to, Ivy. That's no diet, that's hog heaven."

I obviously said what she needed to hear because a grin appears on her face as big as a wide-mouth bass. "Anything and everything you want, Cappygirl. Read some more."

"Well, it says here you can have a dozen eggs and a whole pound of bacon for breakfast if you want it." I shake my head. "That can't be right."

She bobs her head. "But it is."

"Wait a minute. It also says you can chew it up, but you can't swallow it."

"Right again!"

"Well, if you can't swallow it, Ivy Lee, then what do you do with it?"

Ivy Lee yanks out a foil-covered Folger's can from her elephantine pocket-book. The can rattles. "I spit mine in here but you can spit it down the disposal or in the garbage can or wherever. The secret of my fantastic diet is in the chewing, not the swallowing."

"It is?"

"Of course it is! Dieting my way, you get the vitamins and other stuff you need but you don't get the calories. The Spit Diet. Catchy name for it, don't you think so?"

I back up another foot, deliberately averting my eyes from the Folger's can. I don't even want to *think* about what's in there.

"I sho' am glad I ran into you, Cappygirl. You want in on this, don't you?"

"In on what?" I'm feeling dizzy.

"Well, shoot! I'm gonna need a writer for my best selling book, ain't I? Listen. You stick with me and I'll make you a star."

I stare at the grinning lunatic offering to make me famous, and the thought suddenly occurs to me that I am definitely not in the right place at the right time.

"You know something, Ivy? I've been thinking lately that it's about time for me to change career directions. In fact, I'm planning to start out right this minute."

I don't dare look back at her as I charge out of Winn-Dixie at mach speed heading in a new direction.

It's All Greek to Me

"What can be more Southern than to obsess about being Southern?"—Elizabeth Fortson Arroyo

All my life I have been fascinated with Greek Gods and Goddesses, most of whose names I could not pronounce if they threatened to take away my Olympic Medals. Yeah, right. Where I come from people still struggle with English. Nobody speaks Greek and pharmacists don't speak Latin, they only read it.

As for me, I read my daily horoscope in the newspaper, which, if you want to get technical, might be considered token Greek. Hello? The Olympians—get it? I'm not apt to sip my first cup of Starbucks until four small sentences under the heading of *Aquarius* tells me it's okay to do so. Most of the time it doesn't mention coffee, but that's beside the point.

I have no idea why certain Olympian names are attached to certain birth months. Take Taurus the Bull, for instance. What is *that* all about? Everybody knows Taurus is a Ford.

Recently, someone emailed me a bunch of definitive astrological signs with a SOUTHERN slant. I laughed and laughed. I include it in this collection so that you might enjoy it also, and I readily admit that some *other* genius wrote it. Not me. Wish I had.

OKRA (Dec. 22–Jan. 20): Although you appear crude, you are actually very slick on the inside. Okrans have tremendous influence. An older Okran can look back over his life and see the seeds of his influence everywhere. Stay away from Moon Pies.

CHITLIN (Jan. 21–Feb. 19): Chitlins come from humble backgrounds. A Chitlin, however, can make something of himself if he's motivated and has lots of seasoning. In dealing with Chitlins, be careful. They can erupt like Vesuvius. Chitlins relate best with Catfish and Okrans.

BOLL WEEVIL (Feb. 20–Mar. 20): You have an overwhelming curiosity. You're unsatisfied with the surface of things, and you feel the need to bore deep into the interior of everything. Needless to say, you are very intense and driven as if you had some inner hunger. Nobody in their right mind is going to marry you, so don't worry about it.

MOON PIE (Mar. 21–April 20): Moon Pies spend lots of time on the front porch. Their physical appearance is easy to recognize. Big and round are the key words here. They should marry anybody they can get remotely interested in the idea, but it won't be easy. This might be the year for Moon Pies to think about aerobics. Maybe not.

POSSUM (APR. 21–May 21): When confronted with life's difficulties, possums have a marked tendency to withdraw and develop a don't-even-go-there attitude. Sometimes they become so withdrawn, people actually think they're dead. This strategy is probably not psychologically healthy, but seems to work for them.

CRAWFISH (May 22–June 21): Crawfish is a water sign. If a crawfish works in an office, they can always be found hanging around the water cooler. Crawfish prefer the beach to the mountains, the pool to the golf course, the bathtub to the living room. They tend to be not particularly attractive physically, but have very, very good heads.

COLLARD (June 22–July 23): Collards have a genius for communication. They love to get in the "melting pot" of life and share their essence with the essence of those around them. Collards make good social workers, psychologists and baseball managers. As far as their personal life goes, Collards ought to stay away from Moon Pies. It will never work.

CATFISH (July 24–Aug. 23): Catfish are traditionalists in matters of the heart, although one's whiskers may cause a problem or two. Catfish are never easy people to understand. They prefer the muddy bottoms to the clear surface of life. Catfish should definitely stay away from Moon Pies.

GRITS (Aug. 24–Sept. 23): The highest aim of a Grit is to be with others like themselves. They love huddling up with a big crowd of other Grits. They like to travel, and should think about joining a club. Where do they like to go? Anywhere there is cheese, gravy, bacon, butter or eggs. Going places where they have all these things serves them well.

BOILED PEANUT (Sept. 24–Oct. 23): A Boiled Peanut has a passionate desire to help his fellow man. Unfortunately, those who know them best—their friends and loved ones—may find their personality rather salty. Criticism may affect a Boiled Peanut deeply because they are really much softer than they appear. They should go right on ahead and marry anybody they want to because in a certain way, theirs is a charmed life. On the road of life, people will always pull over and stop for Boiled Peanuts.

BUTTER BEAN (October 24–Nov. 22): Butter Beans get along well with everybody and are constantly being invited to all sorts of gatherings. Butter Beans should be proud. They've grown on the vine of life and feel at home no matter what the setting. They can sit next to anybody. However, they, too, should have nothing to do with Moon Pies.

ARMADILLO (Nov. 23–Dec. 21): An Armadillo has a tendency to develop a tough exterior, but are actually quite gentle. A great evening for them might be spent with old friends, a fire, some roots, fruit, worms and insects. They are throwbacks not in the least concerned with today's fashion trends. In fact, they're not concerned with anything about today. They're almost prehistoric in their interests and behavior patterns. They should try to marry up with another Armadillo, but Possum is a somewhat kinky mating possibility.

I don't know about y'all, but all this foreign tawk is making me hungry for a big plate of something strange…like Chitlins and a pan of Fried Okra to go with it.

HOPE COMETH IN THE MORNING

*"Life is not measured by the breaths we take,
but by the moments that take our breath away."*

I eagerly await the last hard freeze of the season when the cold, hard earth wakes up and leaps into spring with blooms that proclaim rebirth. It is then that I throw off my overcoat and wander around outside, astonished at the beauty surrounding me. It is akin to strolling through the Garden of Eden.

Things were not so astonishing when I lived out West. Southern California is overrun with palm trees and bougainvillea, and the hills are alive with the blooms of Magnolias. There are Oaks almost as tall and droopy as if they were grown right here in Georgia. What they don't have, and what I missed seeing the most, were Dogwood trees.

What a culture shock it was for me to discover I was living in a state totally lacking the beauty of a four-cornered, white flowering tree that presents itself each spring in order to remind us of what Easter is all about.

They don't have lightning bugs out there, either. On warm summer nights, I would often gaze out my window in hopes of seeing a lightning bug flicker across the dark sky. I marvel that California kids actually go through an entire childhood without housing lightning bugs in a Dukes Mayonnaise jar with holes punched in the top.

As the spring seasonal changes began to move toward Easter, I always felt emotionally compromised, aching for azaleas and dogwoods mixed on one lawn after another with yellow daffodils. My soul longed for a glimpse of the flowers and trees of the South Carolina Low Country.

The exhibition of colorful azaleas and roses at the Edisto Gardens in the small town where I grew up presented a living painting that surpasses my ability to describe. Monet would have loved it. Every shade, hue and color of Azalea was backed up by countless dogwood trees, robust with blossoms nothing short of dramatic. It was impressive.

Every Easter, the church choirs in the area came together to sing at the Sunrise Service held in the midst of the burgeoning gardens. The flowers, discerning their role in the planned program, managed to slash through the fog of early morning light to deliver hope to those of us waiting for the sunrise.

I was always cold arriving at the gardens, even wearing three layers of clothes underneath my choir robe. Others not in the choir but similarly dressed in layers, moved quietly up the hill hoping to find the best perch on which to listen to the music and hear the message of hope. I remember watching them gather together in the dark, greeting one another with a hug or a handshake and always a smile.

What a magnificent sight when the sun did come up. Standing with other choir members on the slight incline we called a hill, I looked out at a spring bouquet of flowers that stretched over a two-mile radius. It was like looking at a never-ending mural. It was the official nod that welcomed in the new season, rich with the birth of flowers as colorful as Easter Eggs sprouting from grass as green as shamrocks.

We sang, "Up From The Grave He Arose," "In The Garden," "On a Hill Far Away," and other familiar Easter hymns. Friends and neighbors in our little town welcomed Easter while the sun crept up slowly, yawning itself into the newborn day—God's other gift to humankind.

So there you have it—the reason I look forward to the last cold snap, the final week of shivers, socks and sweaters. I'll probably fret about the bulbs I've put in the ground and I'll definitely need to pray for the survival of the already stressed out hydrangeas I bought on sale and planted in the back yard. But in the end, I will rely on things I learned during those cold Easter Sunrise Services.

I will depend on my early conditioning to fill me once again with faith that our garden, as well as our world, will once again burst into bloom. I will see the flicker of lightening bugs from out my window and when the morning comes, I will wake up to azaleas, dogwoods and yellow daffodils.

In the meantime, I'll collect Dukes Mayonnaise jars for my grandkids, who might one day want to teach their children how to catch lightning bugs on warm summer nights.

Weird, Wacky and Beyond Words

"A true friend is someone who thinks that you are a good egg even though he knows that you are slightly cracked."—Bernard Meltzer

Sweet Salty Tears

"Memory is the diary that we all carry about with us."—Oscar Wilde

While visiting recently with a friend from my home town, I asked about his grandson, the one he calls Big Guy.

"Oh, you must mean Blake."

"Yep. That's the one," I said. "Tell me about him."

He put a grandfatherly grin on his face and began to paint a picture of Big Guy.

"I named him Big Guy the first time I laid eyes on him. He was about the size of an aerosol can and I figured he was gonna need a little emotional pumping up from time to time. The name seems to have done the trick. It gives him the idea that we're on the same level, even though he is fully aware that I've got a few years on him, plus a few inches and more than a few whiskers.

When he was old enough to stand by himself, Big Guy and I began to take walks together. At first, they were short jaunts out to the swing set. Occasionally I talked him into going with me to the curb to take out or bring back the garbage cans. He always refused to go after dark, though.

Little by little as he grew, our strolls became more adventurous. On any given day, we might look for frogs on a newly discovered path near the water. At other times, we liked to meander down the dirt road that's in front of my house. On those days, we watched for birds that might have strayed off course while migrating south for the winter. It's a Florida ritual we picked up soon after moving here.

Once, Big Guy even talked his old grandpa into jogging down that same dirt road with him. In practically no time, I was all out of breath and searching frantically for a patch of grass on which to flop my out of shape body. He joined me on the ground after a bit, and together we gazed at the sky and made animal cloud pictures. It didn't last long. That particular day, all he saw in the clouds were white poodles, which bored him right quick.

One special day stands out from all the others in my mind. We had walked down to the water's edge where I showed him how to skip rocks. He was old enough, I thought, for his granddaddy to show him the secret of making a flat rock bounce across water.

'There's an art to this, Big Guy,' I told him. 'It takes practice and a lots of it. But you'll get the hang of it eventually, just like I did. It's a great way to think out your problems.'

On our return home, as we approached the gate leading to the house, Big Guy looked up at me, and in a tiny voice full of trust, he said, 'Granddaddy, will you hold me?'

He was not quite five-years-old and his legs were still trying to catch up with his body. He was tired. There was such a childlike and wondrous quality in his face when he asked me that question, that my heart melted quicker than M&M's can melt in your mouth.

Grinning like crazy, I stooped down to gather up all forty pounds of him, amazed that my back didn't go out. His little body felt as light as one of Mama's scratch biscuits.

I unlatched the gate with my free hand and kicked it closed with my foot, and with Big Guy tucked neatly under my right arm, we headed up the slight incline for home.

I made a big production of sniffing the air. 'Mmmm. Mmmm. You smell that? Smells like Grandma is frying some chicken.'

He smiled and nodded his head. 'Yum. Big Guy loves fried chicken.'

We walked on without saying anything more when I noticed him gazing intently at my face as though seeing something very far away. Feeling silly, I cut my eyes over at him and said, 'Boo!'

He quickly pulled his head back in feigned surprise, a little game the two of us had played hundreds of times before and which always preceded a big, tight hug.

Just as we were coming out of the hug, Big Guy did the sweetest thing. He leaned back into me and very gently rubbed his nose against my whiskers, another "game" we had played since the day he came into my life.

'Granddaddy,' he said softly, 'One of these days when I get big and tall and have lots of whiskers, I will hold *you*.'

Hardly a day goes by now that I don't recall that sweet moment in time with my grandson. It refreshes my soul to think how generously he handed over a little piece of his future to me, with no strings attached.

Now that I am unable to pick him up when he asks me to, or hold him the way I so loved to do in the past, I must be satisfied to relive that moment and enjoy the memory all over again. And each time I do, I feel sweet, salty tears springing from my eyes and rolling freely down into my whiskers as the memory swaddles my heart with love."

Alzenia Pops Her Cork!

"Don't be content with being average. Average is as close to the bottom as it is to the top."—author unknown

Marian does things by the book. Sober as a sow, she is convinced that taking a sip of wine or slow dancing in public, not only makes her splotchy, but it's also a shortcut to hell.

"If I did that, I'd be eternally doomed," she says, emphasizing the doomed part.

Marian is a woman who prefers Emily Dickinson to Sylvia Plath, Law and Order to HBO's Sex and the City, and bottled water to Dom Perignon. Go figure.

"Marian," I tell her, "if you don't have plans to replace the current Anal Retentive Poster Girl, then you might want to lighten up a little bit."

Before I'm done admonishing her, she is shaking her head back and forth, her face turning redder than a summer tomato.

"You just better hush up right now, you hear me? I don't like you to talk that way." Then she adds, "And neither does God."

Marian considers *anal* a four-letter word. This is when I begin to wonder if she could have morphed into my mother right before my eyes.

"I'm not gonna hush, Marian, because I'm worried about you. You're way too uptight and it's unhealthy. You need to take a chill pill, girl."

She tosses her white as grits long hair, cut in a style much too youthful for a woman past her prime. "For your information, my doctor says I am in perfect health."

"Who do you go to? Dr. Doolittle?"

She is putout with me (and not for the first time) for confronting her with a real-life issue, so before I can pull myself up on my high horse again, she quickly changes the subject. I decide to let it go for the time being, knowing full well that one of these days…

*   *   *   *

Three weeks sail by before Marian breaks the silence. She calls to make a lunch date.

She is chronically late, but I long ago learned how to deal with that by arriving late myself. If, by some small miracle, she should arrive at the appointed time and is sitting there waiting for *me*, then I hope I have enough strength left in my body to dial 911. Babe says Marian keeps a running list of excuses she pulls out and uses when she needs to. He may be right.

True to form, she does not show up on time, even after I arrive fifteen minutes late. Eventually, I see her through the window as she bolts out of her car and races into the restaurant. Before scanning the crowded room, she glances at the clock as if to confirm that she has indeed kept me waiting. Her sly smile does not escape my notice.

She pauses in the doorway to stretch her long neck and search for me over the heads of screaming kids throwing chicken fingers, and seniors sipping twenty-five cent coffee.

What looks like a local construction crew waits outside the opened door behind Marian, who leisurely blocks their entry. The men are sweating like pack mules in the 95 degree heat and humidity, their patience becoming obviously thinner with each drop of perspiration. From time to time, their X-rated remarks drift over to where I am seated. Oddly enough, Marian neither blushes nor takes umbrage at the remarks, as I would have expected. She does just the opposite by wheeling around to bless out an overweight roofer who told her (in ungentle-manly terms) to move her well developed tush. It appears that he and his friends need to get back to shagging shingles and don't want to wait one more minute to order a Big Mac.

Marian lifts her chin, looks him straight in the eye, then calmly flips him off. Then, tossing her hair like a teenager, she glides toward me as if on roller blades.

"Marian?" I stammer. "Is that you?"

She quits batting her mascared eyes long enough to let out a throaty giggle. "Marian? Don't be absurd, dahlin'. If I were Marian, I'd still be apologizing to that Neanderthal over there."

I am stunned.

"I don't believe you've had the ples-yah of meeting me," she drawls while stretching out a hand with fingernails longer than a pregnant pause. "I see you snagged us a table. How nice. By the way, I am Alzenia."

Snagged us a table? This is not The Ritz, for heaven's sake, it's McDonald's, where apparently Marian slash Alzenia is now a few fries short of a Happy Meal.

"What have you done to yourself, Marian?" It's almost impossible for me to get past the extra makeup she's wearing, but I have *got* to know.

She breezes by me without even pretending to hear my question. She heads straight over to a table solely occupied by a handsome, middle-aged man. Fluffing her hair, she gives the astonished fellow a broad smile. "It's evah so hot outside, Big Boy, and I'm litrilly dyin' of thirst. You wouldn't mind giving a girl a teensy weensy sip of yo' Co-cola, would you? I just *hate* standing in line."

Like a mesmerized fly caught in a spider web, he picks up the drink and hands it over. "Take all you want," he says in a breathy voice. "In fact, take it all. I don't need it."

She snatches his drink, blows him a kiss, then whirls around and saunters over to where I am standing in line wishing McDonald's had a liquor license. I pointedly pretend that I have never seen her before in my life.

Her lips are painted the color of Gallo Hearty Burgundy and she has applied no less than four coats of Maybelline to her lashes, which she bats at me as if I am George Clooney.

I can ignore her for only so long. "What on God's green earth have you done to yourself, Marian?" I'm wondering if it's time for *her* medication or mine.

"Nuh Uh. Mustn't call me Marian, dahlin'. I told you awlready. My name is Alzenia. Zennie, to my close friends."

"Well then, perhaps you can tell me where *my* close friend is. You must know her. She's the one whose name just happens to be Marian and whose body you have obviously snatched. What have you done to her? You give her back right this minute, do you hear me?"

Alzenia yawns, pulls her long arms up in the air and stretches like a cat. "Oooh, body snatching. Now wouldn't *that* have been worthwhile to write about in my journal. But I'm afraid the reason I'm heah is quite a bit less exciting, deah heart. You see, Marian was being particularly pious this maw-nin' so I ordered her to stay home. Sister Marian can be so capital "B" boring, can't she?"

A Styrofoam voice cuts through my deepening concern.

"Welcome to McDonald's. May I take your order?" I look over to this Marian slash Alzenia slash Zennie person, this woman who only faintly resembles my friend underneath the Mae West facade. "We should order," I say. "What do you want to eat?"

She pushes me aside, leans over the counter close to the cash register and flashes a set of molars that could light up a football stadium. She obviously had her teeth bleached way beyond the Chicklet stage.

"Hey, there, Maria," she says to the Hispanic server, after studying her name badge for a long minute. "How about you go over there and tell that big hunk of a chef to fix me up with a triple Mac. Oh, and *you* can fix *me* an Amaretto shake while he's doing it."

I am now totally convinced that my friend has either been smoking something illegal or tooting something even more illegal.

Maria's mouth opens and a voice that sounds much too computerized says, "Shake flavors are chocolate and vanilla."

"Well, dang it awl," Alzenia whines, before glaring at me as though it's *my* fault.

Glancing back only once, she strides like Sea Biscuit to the door while announcing to the crowded room, "We are soooo outta here. Come, come, come, Dahlin'!"

I stare at her retreating back and stall for only a moment before following along behind her. I don't know where on this small island the woman will ever find an Amaretto Shake, but I would bet Babe's pension that she's *gonna*.

Speaking of Babe, he is *gonna* do some heavy gloating when he adds Alzenia's name to his burgeoning list of my eccentric friends, or as he prefers to call them, The League of Weirdo Women.

Jill of All Trade Schools

"For God's Sake, Mrs. Robinson!"—Benjamin in The Graduate

When it comes to reinventing herself, my friend Jill could write the how-to book. Among other things, she is into metaphysics, so she doesn't see her frequent metamorphoses as anything but normal. She calls it continuing education; I call it neurotic cramming.

"Jill, your learning tree has more branches than Bank of America."

"That's what makes me such an intriguing woman," she retorted. Pushing one side of her wayward blonde hair behind an ear, she gave me a "mind your own business" stare.

The fact that she will buy into every job commercial presented on late night television doesn't bother her one bit. She could have bought a small country with what she has spent learning to be a dental hygienist, doctor's receptionist, building contractor, interior designer, court reporter, travel agent and a whole lot more. Jill is a job junkie.

It all began just after meeting her next door neighbor, a good-looking Cosmo hunk of a guy who was light years younger than Jill. He was single with hair, a young Harvard Business School graduate with bucks—in other words, the man of her dreams.

She looked out her window one day and saw him watering his pansies, which should have been a red flag but sometimes Jill is even blonder than Paris Hilton.

Undaunted, she bolted over to his soggy lawn with the sole intention of getting better acquainted.

"Hi neighbor!" She was Miss Mary Sunshine, all perky and cute. "I'm Jill from next door and I don't believe we've met."

He gave her a look, turned back to the pansies and said, "You're right. We haven't."

I would have turned on my heels and headed straight for the nearest martini bar, but that's me; I don't take rejection well. Hunky Harvard's total lack of interest flew right past our Jolly Jill.

"I'm having people over for drinks on Saturday night," she chirped. "I'd love it if you would join us."

The motor mouth shrugged his shoulders but didn't take his eyes away from the pansies. "I guess so," he mumbled.

At the appointed hour on Saturday, he rang her bell. (Definitely no pun intended.) The only other living souls in her house that night belonged to Kramer, the appropriately name cat, and Crisco, the overweight Poodle with a penchant for peeing on trouser legs.

Knowing full well that she was about to tell him a bald-face lie, she lowered her voice and said, "I hope you don't mind, but everybody else had to cancel. Bad virus going around. No matter…it gives us a chance to get to know each other better. Now. What can I fix you to drink?"

Looking grim, he said, "Sapphire martini. Very dry. Up. Shaken, not stirred of course, and poured into a chilled, 10-ounce martini glass. Two queen olives."

Jill deflated faster than a hot air balloon getting up close and personal with a Stealth Bomber. Sapphire? Chilled martini glass? For Jill, finding two ordinary olives in good condition in her fridge would have been a major challenge.

"Tell you what, dude," she said sweetly while batting her baby blues. "Instead of that, let me pour you a nice glass of chilled wine. It's from right here in South Georgia and the produce manager at The Pig said it was mighty tasty."

The hunk from Harvard bolted out the door as if he had a surface-to-air missile strapped to his tailbone.

That same night, Jill dialed an 800 number to sign up for a course in bartending.

"Never again," she told me, "will I be caught with my pants down," which in my opinion was poor phraseology since the pants down part was her intent from the get-go.

She finished the bartending course, but never got a nickel for tending bar, and for very good reason. She could mix any drink imaginable and even pour it into the proper glass, chilled on request. But she was so slow that a kid celebrating his Bar Mitzvah would graduate from college before Jill could finish mixing his mommy's Cosmopolitan.

After she failed to find even part-time employment as a bartender, she vowed never again to go near another bottle of alcohol or the proper glass in which to pour it.

"I've decided to become a private detective instead," she announced.

"Huh?"

"I signed up for an exciting course I saw on Channel 67. It's called, "Everything You Ever Wanted to Know About Being a Snoop.""

"Gadzooks! Too bad the government doesn't know about that course. Or maybe they do. Still, think of the money they could save by closing down the FBI Academy. They could beat it over to Channel 67 and save the taxpayers big bucks."

"And that's not all. Guess what else? I'm gonna meet a bunch of hunks. Young ones."

I roll my eyes, stifle a giggle and try not to think of pansies. "Well, good luck with that, Jill. Just don't serve them any South Georgia wine."

She cocked her head. "Your sarcastic remark tells me you are just plain jealous of my exciting life and the pile of money I'm gonna earn once I'm a full-fledge detective with a license and everything."

"You're not going to be carrying a gun, are you?"

She sniffed. "Well, not at first, but I'm sure in time that can be arranged."

I keep wondering if there is a bartending refresher course she might consider taking. We would all be so much better off getting hammered than having to deal with Jill when she's packing heat.

THE SUNNY SIDE OF THE STREET

*"And by and by Christopher Robin came to an end of things,
and he was silent, and he sat there, looking out over the
world just wishing it wouldn't stop."*—*A.A. Milne*

Entirely too much time has passed since I visited the mother of my childhood friend. I look at the diminutive woman seated across from me and marvel that at eighty-four years old, her unlined face shows not a trace of sorrow or sadness. Her smile is wide, her eyes brighter than mine, her laughter is a violin lightly plucking at the strings of my heart.

"I remember the day we first laid eyes on you," she says, as a mischievous glint appears in her old eyes. Thus begins a story told and retold for most of my life, yet one I never tire of hearing.

"Your family had just moved to town." She grins. "But we hadn't met y'all yet. My chirren were in the backyard playing when all of a sudden Dickie let out an awful scream. Like to scared me to death."

She looks at me, shakes her head and in a pretty good imitation of two-year-old Dickie, says, "Huh hit me on my head wit' th' cat!"

Contrite even after all these years, I feel the color of embarrassment as it slowly crawls up my face.

"Law…I looked up to where the child was pointing and saw *you* for the first time ever. When I asked who you were and where you had come from, the other kids said they didn't know, that you just wandered up."

She cocks her head to the side and purses her lips into a tight smile. "I stood there trying to figure out what I should do with you when I saw a lady walking toward the house. It was your mama, of course, looking for you all over the place. Child, you were just a baby, yet you crossed that big street all by yourself as soon as you heard the other kids playing. I reckon you wanted to play, too."

I was three-years-old at the time and from what I've been told, it would not be the last time I wandered off from the home fires. "So how come I hit Dickie with that mechanical cat I've been hearing about all these years?"

She shakes her head. "Who knows? You had hold of it. He wanted it. You had no intention of giving it to him and that was that. It was the day you and Peggy began your life-long friendship. People always thought y'all were cousins. And your mama, bless her heart, and I became friends for life, too."

This beautiful lady sighs contentedly and shifts slightly in her straight-back chair, a necessity since her recent lumbar surgery. The almost imperceptible movement is as close as she will come to a complaint of any kind.

We speak of family, both hers and mine. We talk of my grandchildren and her grands and great-grands. She digs out a shoebox full of wedding pictures and babies born to people I have yet to meet. She tells me how happy she is in her new living space at The Home, and how lucky for her that there is a screen door she can open anytime she wants to feel a nice cross-breeze.

We don't talk about Peggy, my very first friend, gone now nearly ten years. The pain is too raw for us both. My gaze drifts from time to time to the same picture of Peggy that sits atop my desk at home, but still, neither of us broaches the subject. Instead, I ask about Peggy's youngest son.

She laughs out loud. "That boy will never change. Why, he could tee-tee on your foot and make you believe it was raining." She laughs some more. "But he'll yank the shirt off his back and give it to you if you say you like it, then hug you so hard you'll beg for mercy."

So much like his mother, I think, and draw in a breath. "He was in Seattle with Peggy when she went for a bone marrow transplant, as was I. That boy was so concerned about his mother. We all were."

My other mother looks down quickly and I fear I've opened a wound not yet healed and I'm immediately remorseful. She looks back up at me and for a moment, we share the depth of our sorrow and our need for closure.

"My Peggy was such a brave girl. She so hated having to give up. Because of her though, we all learned a thing or two about courage, didn't we?"

I catch my breath again and hold it inside. I do not want to cry in front of this stalwart woman who has buried a son, a daughter, a husband. Who only three

years ago survived the incredibly invasive Whipple Procedure for pancreatic cancer. Who smiles at and speaks to every person she meets while pushing her walker
down the narrow Hallway of The Home. I know precisely where Peggy got her
courage.

Stooping down, I give her an awkward hug and a light kiss on her rose-petal
cheek. "I'll come back to see you soon," I say.

"Well then, we'll catch up some more another time," she replies.

I nod my head, but my heart tells me that there will probably not be another
time. Not for the two of us. Only after her door has closed softly behind me do I
allow my well of tears to bathe my sad, sad soul.

PISTOL PACKING PATTY

"Suppose they gave a war, and no one came?"—Leslie Parrish-Bach

I can see Patty's mouth moving, but the roar of her Humvee obliterates the sound of her words. I'm no good at lip reading so I have to strain to snatch even a piece of her ongoing chatter.

"Civilians call 'em Hummers." Patty shouts in my direction. "But not me, Babycakes. I call my ride a Humvee."

Her "ride" is doing something, but I wouldn't go so far as to say it's humming.

Incredibly, Patty shelled out way over sixty-five thousand big ones for this ugly piece of pink metal. Pink. She ordered it special. She could have bought a fabulous looking Jag for the same money, and it would have been fully equipped with real leather seats, power everything, CD and DVD player *and* a GPS.

Shifting gears as though doing her thang at a Daytona NASCAR gig, she passes a pokey little Corvette at such close range that I see my reflection in the driver's Raybans. My heart drops down somewhere near my kneecaps and I think it may choose to stay put.

"For heaven's sake, Patty. Slow down," I shout at my five-foot tall, daredevil friend behind the wheel. She is perched on a child's booster stool, the only thing that allows her to see over the dash without standing up.

She takes her eyes off the road long enough to throw me a look and my heart does the kneecap thing again. "Keep your eyes on the freaking road, Patty and slow down!"

"I drive fast because I am seated behind the wheel of a HUMVEE." Without even a glance in the rearview mirror, she charges past a Mobil Oil tanker truck the size of a 747, which makes my liver do a shag step before it joins my heart down around my knees.

Patty was sixty-something years old on her last birthday. Looking at her, she is the perfect picture of a sweet little old lady, somebody's very short grandmother. She dresses in size three, wrinkle-free pants and extra-small tee shirts with tiny, embroidered flowers on the front. Having discovered Reeboks trimmed in pink as soon as her aging feet began to grow odd-shaped bumps and knots, since then she has never been tempted by Nike Airs or Nike anything else. Patty maintains a modicum of style only in the sense that her polyester pantsuits always match her Reeboks.

Her once flaming red hair faded to white long ago, but she and Miss Clairol put their heads together and came up with a pale pink tint, leaving two inches of white streaking down the middle of her head. Think pink skunk.

We swerve into Peaches Service Center in order for the Humvee to guzzle enough gasoline to fuel a fleet of Fords for an entire year, and I am finally comfortable enough to release the breath I have been holding in.

"Hey, Babycakes, catch that windshield for me while I pump." Her voice booms official enough to make me jump out and nearly break my leg. It takes only ten seconds for me to realize that I will need an extension ladder to "catch" the windshield. In fact, I will need to stand on a nearby trashcan just to haul my butt back into the car/tank.

I give up quickly and crawl back inside the Humvee. As I reach for my seat belt, my fingers wrap around a cylinder of cold metal instead of the expected safety harness. Puzzled, I turn around to see what it is, and that's when I nearly fall out of the car/tank once again. I jerk my hand away and scream. "Patty! There's a weapon of mass destruction in this tank!"

My mind is racing faster than Patty's manic drive down the causeway. I have never actually laid eyes on an AK-47 before, but I'm pretty sure my well-manicured fingers have just been up close and personal with my first one. I can't think of any reason for the sweet little lady from Ludiwici to be flitting around South Georgia in a pink military vehicle complete with an assault weapon strapped to the back of the passenger seat.

Patty clunks the gas nozzle down, slides her card through the slot and in less than forty seconds, leaps back into the Hummer as thought she is Special Ops with immediate attack orders direct from Rummy.

She glances over at me. "Your face is as white as a mashed potato." She says this casually while firing up the engine and simultaneously drowning out all sound within a five-mile radius.

I blink once and casually reach over and snatch the Humvee's key out of the ignition, simultaneously killing the noise and temporarily restoring peace—if not globally, at least within the aforementioned five-mile radius.

"We are not moving one inch until you explain to me why there is an assault weapon strapped to the back of my seat." She looks at me as though I am a very slow child.

"Oh, fudge. It's not real." She puts a sly grin on her face. "Ha! Fooled *you* though, didn't it? That baby is also guaranteed to fool the enemy."

"Enemy? And just what enemy would that be, Patty?"

She rolls her eyes. "Duh! We're fighting a War on Terror. Haven't you heard?"

"Yes, Patty, I heard. But it is being fought in the Middle East, *not* in Georgia—or haven't *you* heard?"

"Duh. The War on Terror is everywhere and I, along with Homeland Security, plan to be ready to rock n' roll and kick some butt if and when we face the enemy."

I close my eyes as a mental image fills my head. Tee-niney Patty is pointing her toy assault weapon at a bearded, turban-doffed terrorist who has a bomb basted to his belly. It is not a pretty picture.

"That's right, Patty. You go ahead and aim a fake AK-47 at a terrorist. Be sure to do it while you're perched on your Billy Barty booster chair behind the wheel of this gawd-awful pink Hummer. You'll kill him for sure, because he'll die laughing after he blows your butt to kingdom come."

She lets out a turbo charged breath then throws the slow child look at me once again. "HumVEE. It's called a HumVEE. Why can't you get that straight?"

Snatching the keys out of my hand, within seconds she fires up the engine. "I'm a patriot and I gotta do what I gotta do, Babycakes. Besides, I can't get a permit for a real AK-47. They're gonna be real sorry when Chuck Heston gets my letter of complaint."

She shoots out of Peaches and onto Highway 17 while I grit my teeth and hold on for dear life to the side of the pink Humvee/Hummer. She may look like a sweet little lady from Ludiwici, but the truth is, Ol' Patty is packing heat—even if the only time it shows up is in the form of a flaming Hot Flash.

Attack of the Polka Dotters

"If stupidity got us into this mess, then why can't it get us out?"—*Will Rogers*

A loud sigh whooshes through the telephone receiver after I ask Arlene how she has been doing. It makes me think maybe a tornado is fixing to touch down.

"I declare," she says. "I'm nothing but a wuss when it comes to saying no."

I might as well ask her what she's talking about. Otherwise, I'll be stuck on the phone for the next hour and a half.

"What's up, girlfriend?"

Another tornado sound whooshes through the phone line. "Do you remember that polka dot scarf you gave me for Christmas?"

"Uh huh."

"Well, I wore it yesterday. It went real good with the new yellow hat I bought special. Just for the meeting."

"Oh? What meeting was that?"

"You know. The Dotters. We had a brunch."

Please, lord, don't let her get started on that subject. When she first told me about the Polka Dot Sisterhood she was asked to join, it sounded as though she had found a home, and I was happy for her.

"You won't believe what happened."

"Try me," I say while silently thanking Ma Bell for portable phones. I plop down in the nearest chair and switch on CNN with no sound.

"The brunch was held at Shirley's house. She was one of the original Polka Dotters, you know. She organized it and all, and she's the one who got *me* in."

"Uh huh." The fact that Squirrelly Shirley talked a bunch of women into calling themselves Polka Dotters doesn't surprise me a bit.

"I said I'd make the centerpiece for Shirley's table, and she seemed to be real happy about that. I love her to pieces, but she doesn't know a daisy from a dandelion. Lord knows *what* she would have stuck in the middle of that table."

"Probably something silk," I say and flip to Oprah on Channel 3.

"You're absolutely right and I'd have been mortified. Anyhoo, I thought my idea of a summer seaside theme would be perfect since we live on an island and all."

Oprah's guest today is The Coupon Queen. She's telling everybody how much money she saved since she started clipping in 1985. Now she's hell-bent on hawking the book (probably ghost written) about her life and how clipping coupons has made her a household name.

Arlene draws a breath but keeps right on talking. "I worked my fingers to the bone on that centerpiece. Why, it took me fourteen hours and twenty-three minutes to fashion little palm trees out of potatoes, carrots and bell peppers. I was really inspired."

The Coupon Queen is as compelling as Arlene's veggie trees. I flip to Judge Judy who is in the middle of throwing the book at an ignorant looking couple who tried to trade grandma in for a riding lawn mower.

"I took my Barbie doll that I got for my thirteenth birthday, set her down in the middle of the table on top of a beige lace doily that kinda-sorta looked like sand. I stuck one of those cute little Piña Colada umbrellas next to Barbie. We can't let her get too much sun, you know." She starts to giggle like she just chuga-lugged four little Piña Coladas. "It was so authentic, 'and the little vegetable palm trees made it even better. I swear I could hardly tell the difference between them and the real ones."

Some people I know really need to get a life. I switch to Crossfire on CNN.

"I dressed Barbie up in a polka dot mid-drift top, hot pink shorts and a big yellow hat just like mine. Oh, and I also made a sail boat from a melon rind and filled it with pinkish red melon balls and passion fruit."

"Of course you did," I murmur.

The little twerp with the bow tie on Crossfire has argued himself into a state that looks a whole lot like a hissy fit. I stifle a yawn while Arlene, the modern day Donatello, continues droning on about her altruistic creative brilliance.

"I whipped up a rum dip, too, and placed it inside the center of a purple cabbage, just to be different. It's good to be different, don't you think so?"

"Um hmmm."

"Shirley contributed a quiche, which I'm sure came from the frozen food section at Winn-Dixie. She sliced a few tomatoes and cucumbers, and then *microwaved* some Jimmy Dean sausage biscuits. I saved the day, I want you to know, with the chocolate covered strawberries that I stayed up till way after midnight dipping by hand."

The devil himself pulls the next words from my lips. "Arlene, are you and Shirley doing drugs? If not, then does the Polka Dot Oath require you to eat like truck drivers whacked out on Wacky Tabacky?"

"Oh no, nothing like that. Normally, we just go to Shoney's and get the salad bar. I thought it would be nice to do something special, even though Shirley made it plain to everybody that she didn't think it was necessary."

The light begins to dawn. "Arlene, let me ask you something. Did Shirley call you up and thank you for all the wonderful things you made for her brunch?"

"Well, no, not exactly."

I grab the TV remote and flip the off button. "What exactly does *not exactly* mean?"

She clears her throat. "It means that she isn't exactly speaking to me at all, that's what. And that's why I'm so upset! You'd think she would have 'preshated what I did, wouldn't you? Those vegetable palm trees took me forever to carve out."

The light dawns completely. "Shirley kicked you out of the Polka Dot Sisterhood, didn't she?"

Arlene does the tornado whoosh through the phone again. "Just until hell freezes over."

SCOUT'S HONOR

Honor: honesty and integrity in one's beliefs and actions.—BSA Pledge

Today Babe and I have the honor of taking a tour through the Mighty Eighth Air Museum near Savannah. Our guide is a personal friend who has immersed us in the legacies left us by men who dared to believe; men with integrity; men with honor.

Lt. General E.G. "Buck" Shuler has been my friend since we were kids. He is the Chairman of the Board of Trustees for the Museum. I am a captive audience while the General speaks of a significant fighter plane, or points to a picture of a celebrated Ace. He wears a crown of white hair nowadays, but I can still see him as the redheaded boy he used to be.

At fifteen, maybe sixteen years old, Buck's tall, lanky body is erect. He holds his chin high as the Scout Master pins a red, white and blue BSA medal over my friend's heart. Having earned his twenty-first merit badge, he is being elevated to Eagle Scout. Future leader. A man who will one day make a difference.

The expressions I see on the faces of his parents reflect the pride they feel in their son's early accomplishments. They know how hard it was for him to earn merit badges while juggling schoolwork, football and a popular student's social life. They are raising their son to be unafraid of challenges, to honor commitments and to do his best always. Buck's mother and father gave him a caring heart and soul, and they are especially proud of that endowment.

Someone in the group behind me sneezes and I am quickly brought back to the here and now as my old friend tells us about the gallant Mighty Eighth men who have served our country since I was two-years-old. Proud and happy to credit his compatriots, he pointedly shies away from mentioning his own, not insignificant contributions.

Buck Shuler, outstanding graduate of The Citadel and former Commander of the Eighth Air Force, was first a dedicated Boy Scout. It occurs to me that his early training likely cemented and honed his sense of commitment. Perhaps that Boy Scout base of knowledge brought him to leadership positions at The Citadel and continued to guide him toward an illustrious military career. For sure, it reminded him to do his best, to do his duty to God and country, and to always help others.

This former Boy Scout flew 107 combat missions over North Vietnam, the Republic of Vietnam and Laos while I went about my daily routine tucking two baby boys safely into bed each night. My son's first day in kindergarten occurred right about the same time Buck was deployed to Taegu Air Base, South Korea due to the USS Pueblo crisis.

My children and I loved to meander along the South Carolina beaches all summer in search of shark's teeth. While my friend was flying F-4C combat support missions along the Korean demilitarized zone, I looked for shells, went to parties and took my freedom for granted.

On the days and nights that I read the latest novel all safe and sound at home, or fussed at my husband for squeezing the toothpaste tube in the middle, Buck was initiating the first air attack on Saddam Hussein in the Persian Gulf.

Because of his strong determination, strength of character and knowledge, it is now possible for people who have taken peace for granted—people like me—to honor the brave men and women who serve in our stead. Buck Shuler would be the last one to tell you that he was a key player in the formation of this Mighty Eighth Air Museum, but he was. And he did it in order to honor those who did *not* take peace for granted.

My friend richly deserves his Distinguished Service Medal with Oak Leaf Cluster, his Legion of Merit with Oak Leaf Cluster, the Distinguished Flying Cross, Air Medal with five Oak Leaf Clusters, and his Air Force Commendation Medal with Oak Leaf Cluster. He more than earned the Republic of Korea Order of National Security Merit Cheonsu Medal, as well as thirteen other decorations and ribbons.

If, however, all of the medals, citations and awards presented to this honorable man throughout the years should somehow disappear, never to be seen again by the naked eye, I suspect that one imprint would remain stamped forever on his brain. It would be a red, white and blue BSA Eagle Scout medal, pinned over his heart in 1952. It would be faded from the many years of service given to other future leaders who have learned from him what it takes and what it means to make a difference.

My friend General E. G. "Buck" Shuler, Eagle Scout, soars like an eagle in my book. Scout's Honor.

SEPTEMBER SONG FOR A BUTTERFLY

"There is nothing in a caterpillar that tells you it's going to be a butterfly."—Buckminster Fuller

I learned recently that a very dear man, an old poet I once knew, had died. This morning I woke up remembering the day I met him.

The man was seated with his wife at a writing workshop I was attending. I noticed them I think, because there was a shine surrounding them both, a shine like a patina, and it was what caused me to look at them until my curiosity could stand it no longer.

I turned to the woman next to me. "Who are those two old people sitting by themselves on the front row?"

"That's R.B. and Lidie Cahill," she whispered." She rolled her eyes as if to say that anybody with a grain of sense would know *that*.

"They're a regular fixture around here at this seminar," she added. "Every summer they drive down from North Carolina because this is where they met and fell in love. Isn't that just about the sweetest thing you ever heard?"

About that time, R.B. approached the podium and began to read a humorous poem he had penned. He talked like he laughed—as if he constricted his vocal chords on purpose, twanging his "A's" like hill people often do. When R.B. said something that began with an "A," it came out flat, like when you say "that fat cat." Gomer Pyle talked like that, too.

I later learned that he enjoyed telling tall tales on himself. I once heard him say, "One time Lidie said to me, 'R.B., you just go look at yo'sef in the mirror 'cause you got chocklit ice cream stuck in your mustache.' I laughed real hard when I saw it dripping off my chin onto my new shirt that I'd paid a whole bunch of money for. So I told Lidie, 'This would make a right good story.' Haw. Haw."

R.B.'s laugh, if not always his tall tales, was infectious.

When he wasn't wearing chocolate, he often sported long muttonchops that curved around his long face. That type of sideburn could not have been more suitable for him because it framed a ruddy complexion that turned a deeper red by the time it reached his pencil-straight nose. Every time R.B. smiled, that nose of his joined up with his lips and crawled up his face like the two were in cahoots, as indeed they were. Still grinning, he would then take his index finger and push his silver rimmed glasses back up to where they belonged. He had to do that quite a lot, I noticed, since he smiled so often. I never heard him whistle, but all the years that I knew him, I kept expecting him to walk into a room, his lips poised in whistle mode and tweeting a melody. Happy, contented men seem to always whistle, I've noticed.

R.B. didn't just wear bright pink trousers, he *headlined* them. His royal blue suspenders topped off either a black or pink Polo shirt that he buttoned all the way up to his Adam's Apple. I'll bet his Polo shirts were the only concession to popular trends he was ever willing to make. R.B. was a man way past caring about fashion statements—he made his *own* declarations and he made no bones about it.

You have to admire a man like that.

He was a born romantic with an innate sense of how to make his woman feel special. He was so loving and gentle around Lidie that it made my heart swell. It looked to me like he wanted to touch her as often as possible, if only with an occasional tap. I often noticed him as he listened to the words of another poet. After a while, he would lean in closer and closer to Lidie until his slightly smiling face had brushed up next to her silver hair, just behind her ear. Pretty soon, not hurriedly or without thinking, R.B. would kiss that little section of her hair. It was ever so gentle and Lidie, apparently accustomed to his loving ways, barely blinked. But she noticed.

It was easy to see that their devotion to one another stretched beyond that which had been carved out over the years of living together as man and wife. They had been joined as one long enough to compliment one another like Gainsborough's Blue Boy and Pinky.

When Lidie began to lose her hearing, R.B.'s ears became her ears. Much like the tender kiss he often planted on her hair, Lidie scarcely noticed the transition. I doubt that either one of them were ever consciously aware of her hearing loss. They functioned as one finely tuned, well-oiled piece of people machinery, the kind that automatically slides into place at the first sign of a glitch.

His old eyes became even weaker toward the end, making it necessary for him to wear thicker glasses and also to squint. But if anybody were to ask me, I would tell them that even with poor vision, R.B. Cahill was able to see beyond pink pants, blue suspenders, hearing losses and time ticking away much too fast. This unique human being had learned somehow to peer deeply into the souls of others.

Maybe it was that very quality that gave him the special smile he wore—a grin that seemed to emerge from a cocoon spun of sheer joy and unconditional love. It was a grin that crawled like a caterpillar all over his innocent, child-like face to finally morph into a flawless, beautiful laugh that might have come from a butterfly, if a butterfly only knew how to laugh.

THE SAVING GRACE

*"Old age is when former classmates are so gray,
wrinkled and bald, they don't recognize you."—Anonymous*

My high school class reunion is in full swing and here I stand in the middle of the room, surrounded by a bunch of people I sat next to, or shared a class with, for twelve of my much younger years. Would I recognize them if we passed each other on the street? I don't think so.

For instance, my friend Annie told me that the woman over by the window is none other than Jean Marie Smith. Annie must be mistaken. That woman is way too old and out of shape to be the Prom Queen we all loved to hate.

My mind is temporarily bogged down on Memory Lane when I feel three sharp taps on my shoulder. Turning around quickly, I come face-to-face with an old man standing way too close and grinning like he just discovered Viagra. The scary thing is, he looks vaguely familiar.

"Hey there!" I smile big as you please, pretending to know who he is.

"Don't you 'Hey there' me, girl! I came over here for a big ol' hug." His larger than life hands swoop around me and pull me into a Goliath Grip. "I swear to my soul you look good enough to eat. Yessiree, bobtail."

Recognition hits me like a two-by-four between the eyes. The old codger hugging the daylights out of me is none other than Jimmy Clyde Lewis. Had there been senior superlative categories for Most Un-popular, Most Obnoxious, Most Un-attractive, Least Athletic, Worst Dancer and Least Likely to Succeed, ol' Jimmy Clyde would have gone down in high school history.

He squeezes me again and I think he splintered one of my ribs. I cry out and try to loosen his hold on me but he squeezes tighter. His nose is almost touching mine.

"Lemme take a close look at you, girl." He must have eaten every deviled egg on the burgeoning buffet table. His breath makes my eyes burn.

"Show me your ring finger," he commands. "Please God don't let her be wearing no little band o'gold." My wedding ring glares back at him. Thank goodness I remembered to dip it in ammonia before leaving the house. He blanches as though he's been hexed.

I snatch my hand away from the old coot and proceed to dazzle him with a ten-karat smile. "That's right, bubba, so back off."

And he does. Thank you, God.

A giggle sifts its way through the surrounding noise and I turn around to find a woman who looks old enough to be her own mother. That said, I would like to pin a freaking medal on the genius that invented the nametag.

"Mary Linn? Is that you?"

She giggles again before stepping forward with her arms outstretched. This time I respond in kind. It has been forty something years since we've seen each other, and it appears that the word diet has not been a frequent topic of conversation around her house in all that time.

She steals the next half hour from me by talking about every inconsequential thing her grandchildren have ever done or not done. I remember Mary Linn as a detail sort of person, but having to listen to the Social Security numbers of all seven of her grands is more information than politeness demands.

The minute she stops to take a breath, I jump in like Esther Williams in a 1955 swim film. "I've got five grandkids from hell."

As soon as the words leave my lips, she shrinks away from me in hysterical panic, backing off as if for protection. Hands that only moments ago patted me with affection are now pointed fingers that threaten my eyeballs.

"Those chirren gotta be saved," she shrieks. "They gotta find Jesus before it's too late. The Rapture is coming and it won't be long now."

I back away from her as though she has explosives strapped to her very sizable waist. Lord, have mercy. The woman took me seriously. "Oh, Mary Linn wait a minute. You've got it all wrong. Let me explain…"

She covers her ears with both hands, squeezes her eyes shut and shakes her head back and forth. "I cain't and won't listen to another blasphemous word from your sinful lips." Then her voice takes on a whispery tone. "I will pray for your little ones, though, seed of your own flesh and blood." She opens her eyes wide. "I'll pray that Satan be flushed from their lives, and I'll begin right now. Right this minute. Won't you join me as I kneel and plead for the souls of your little grandchirren."

Dropping to her knees, she mutters what I assume is a prayer, although I wouldn't place any bets on it. The incomprehensible language known as speaking in tongues has always puzzled me. I back off fast in hopes of getting out of her sight before she opens her eyes and calls up a snake handler.

How on earth could this woman be the same person who showed me how to roll a joint? The same Mary Linn who was better known as Mary Sinn? Holy Cow! That's what I call one humdinger of a metamorphosis.

Pretty soon, I find myself eyeball to eyeball with David, yet another old classmate. I am badly in need of a dry double martini and I don't give a hoot if every born again Baptist or snake handler in the county knows it.

David was the quietest fellow in our class and so shy he was almost invisible. I don't think many of us ever noticed him. I know I didn't. Well, that is far from the case today. My oh my. How things do change.

The good looking, hunky face I'm gazing at is graced with large, sympathetic, Omar Shariff liquid brown eyes. I am torn between staring at him and looking for the martini of my dreams. I decide to do both. My voice is steeped in angst when I blurt, "Oh, Gawd, David. You look like somebody who takes a drink. Please tell me I'm right."

Laughing out loud, he nods his head. "I drink like a fish. Just ask my wife, Grace Ann. I was chilling out on the porch with a bourbon and branch when she noticed you were having what appeared to be an uncomfortable little chat with Saint Mary Linn. Grace Ann told me I better get my butt in here pronto and rescue you."

I glance over his right shoulder in hopes of spotting Grace Ann so I can wave and blow her a grateful kiss.

"She's the one holding the martini glass," he says, grinning all over himself.

Like it says in the Bible, "By grace, ye shall be saved."

Praise the Lord!

Help! I'm Talking and I
Can't Shut Up!

*"My mother used to say that there are no strangers,
only friends you haven't met yet. She's now in a maximum
security twilight home in Australia."*—Dame Edna Everage

Babe hates it when I talk to strangers. He predicts that one of these days I'll befriend another Charlie Manson, bring him home and introduce him to my single girlfriends.

"But, Babe," I tell him, "I enjoy talking to people. I've met some of my best friends standing in lines at airports or biding my time somewhere in a foreign country. Take Claudia, for instance."

A few years ago, I was stretched out on a poolside lounge chair at a resort in Malaysia, wondering what a nice girl like me was doing in a place like Kuala Lumpur. Homesick as a puppy, I longed to hear the sound of a familiar voice. I was trying to read a book, but the words were blurry from the perspiration that methodically dripped onto the pages. The ice in my exotic, rum-based coconut something-or-other drink melted long before the drink ever touched my lips. The sun above me delivered equator strength rays that blistered my skin before I could slather on enough sunscreen to do a piece of good.

Having turbo sighed at least half a dozen times, I was slowly sinking into more of my misery when I heard a loud splash. It was followed by a shower of chlorinated water that covered me from head to pink toenail polish and completed the blurring job on my book.

"Woo-hoo! This feels rat nice!"

I jerked my head up in time to see a woman frolicking in the pool, seemingly without a care in the world. Grinning like a chessie cat, she spoke a loud version of Southerneze. Having checked out the other sunbathers, mostly Asian, she apparently figured that nobody would comprehend her unique language. Haw! In less time than it takes to blink, I shouted out to her.

"Hey! Where you from?" By this time I had hoisted my broiling body off the lounge chair and was leaning over the edge of the pool.

"Texas! I'm from Texas, honey." Her grin was a wide one and what a mouthful of teeth she had. "How 'bout chew?"

"Get outta that pool, girl," I commanded. "We gotta tawk."

What occurred next was my first but not last conversation with Claudia. It was a sisterhood at first sight. Since that time, I have seen her only once, and most likely I would not recognize her if she swam back into my life today. But we write to one another on an irregular basis. When I hear from her, I immediately stop whatever I'm doing and rip into her letter. She writes funnier and more entertainingly than anyone I know.

Just the other day, she wrote me.

"Dear Girlfriend," she began.

"I continue to preserve and put up in jars anything that cannot move faster than I do. So far, that amounts to blackberries, wild grapes, figs, pickles, plums, two very young grandchildren and the Hispanic yardman, Alfredo Gonzales.

"In my spare time, I have also been running the usual summer resort sans staff, of course. We were blessed with houseguests for twenty-seven straight days and nights, interrupted only once when I ran away to New York City for four days. I took my granddaughter, which may not have been a wise decision, given my state of mind at the time. I am still recovering from all of the above. I'm too freaking old for this nonsense.

"At present, my beloved Bubba is seeing a doctor for a 'head' problem of some sort. I pray daily: Please Jesus, send tranquilizers, uppers, downers, anti-depressants, whatever it takes. Oh, they're not for him. They're for me. I need them. I want them. Nobody listens to me.

"More of this disgusting saga later. Love to you from Claudia."

Claudia was married to a petroleum man at the time we met. When his gas ran out, so did she. She then married a Texas rancher named Bubba. He moved her from what she had considered a civilized existence in Houston, to the outskirts of a small Texas town named Saltlick. Claudia somehow missed the clue that her cowpoke husband wanted her to become a cowpoke wife.

Several years ago, Claudia, like so many bored women of a certain age, attempted to hit upon that one special thing that would define her existence and give meaning to her home on the range life.

She wrote: "I have finally discovered my true gift, girlfriend. I'm about to start my own business designing and creating belts, purses and anything else I can think of. Out of what, you ask? Alligator hides and rattlesnake skins."

The wee small fact that gators were on the endangered list at the time did not wilt her enthusiasm or deter her creativity. She high-tailed it down to South America and came home loaded with stinking reptile skins. Fashioning purses, belts and even dog collars from them, she proceeded to sell every one. Neiman Marcus pesters her even today for more of the same. Go figure.

Claudia is a multi-faceted woman with the attention span of a silk plant with A.D.D. The skin game got to her eventually so next I heard, she had gone on to something else which apparently has made Bubba boot clicking happy. He sorely missed having a good woman up in the Big House who was capable of handling the intricacies of his infrequent Texas Barbeques.

I adore this woman and her raucous sense of humor. I can't imagine not getting the occasional letter from Claudia. I might have pitched a fit the day she dove into the pool in Kuala Lumpur and ruined my sexy novel. I might have stormed back to the hotel in a huff instead. But then, I would have missed meeting this funny, irreverent woman.

Babe says I'm going to get in trouble talking to strangers, that I should be careful. But more often than not, those strangers end up enriching my life almost as much as Claudia has done over these twenty-something years. Having her for a friend who entertains me with her letters is like having flowers delivered to my door all the way from Saltlick, Texas just when I least expect it.

War Paint and
Wrinkles

*"Eve nibbled on that apple because the serpent promised
it would make her smart. If he'd said, 'It will erase fine
wrinkles,' she would have buzzed through the Tree of
Knowledge like a beaver."—Author Paula Wall*

Georgia Faye's hair is whiter than a milk-fed chicken and she tosses it like she's a 1940's sex symbol, Rita Hayworth style. Reaching up with both hands, she "combs" through it lovingly with her short, unpolished nails. A smug, self-satisfied expression settles over her makeup-free face.

"I *adore* my hair. I can't go anywhere, even to a garage sale, that people don't comment on how beautiful it is."

Georgia Faye is fixated on her crown of white, which only recently has been allowed to bask in the light of day. Up until now, the real color was something only her closest friends knew for sure. She was very often caught wearing a dead white streak close to her scalp, which would widen with each breath she took, a signal that she was overdue for an afternoon with her other best friend, Miss Clairol.

I shrug my shoulders. "Goodness gracious, Georgia Faye, that white hair of yours sho' gives you a rush, doesn't it."

"You don't like my hair?"

"Now, what makes you ask a question like that?"

She tut, tut, tuts a few times, then gives me The Look. "I know you don't like it. It's written all over your face!"

I snort. "Those are not words you see written on my face, Georgia Faye. Those are wrinkles with interesting conversational possibilities."

Georgia Faye and I went to high school together. We sat next to each other in chorus class, participated in daylong talkathons, and we still do. She introduced me to my first husband, not that I hold it against her or anything. The bottom line is, we have seen each other through weddings, babies, kindergarten, divorces, PMS and menopause. Even so, every time she fluffs those white locks of hers, I need to remind myself that she is *not* her own grandmother.

I admit it. White hair did *not* make the top ten list of things I wanted to have when I grew up. White hair on women my age creeps me out. It's pre-everything I ever learned at my mother's knee. Embracing the white hair mentality is tantamount to thumbing my nose at the tiny dab of progress made by repressed women throughout history.

"You could make your life a whole lot easier if you didn't color your hair," Georgia Faye declares suddenly. "At your age, blonde hair and pony tails are not only inappropriate, they just don't work for you. And you should also give some thought to not being a slave to the makeup counter at Belk's."

I lift my defiant chin. "I haven't worn a pony tail in two whole years."

She squints her eyes and, as if accusing me of treason, says, "You're still blonde, aren't you? Period. Paragraph."

I glare at my white-haired friend who is wearing no makeup, clean white socks and a pair of bright red, polyester stretch pants, circa 1968. Underneath the heavily starched dress shirt she rescued from the Goodwill pile three years ago, she has on a pastel polyester Tee shirt with embroidered roses across the chest. She brags to people that she buys her clothes at the store where America shops. Georgia Faye's chances of becoming a fashion maven at her age are between zero and nil, but somewhere in the world there's bound to be a cartoon waiting to be drawn of her. Move over, Maxine.

Her suggestion to me that my life could be easier without touch-ups gives me momentary pause. For one nanosecond, I'm tempted to let it all hang out and the rest drag. No crash diets, no overspending at the Clinque counter, no getting out of breath while squeezing into skin-tight designer jeans. No Miss Clairol…

No Miss Clairol? What's up with you, Miz High Maintenance, my "other" self screams in my ear. *Have you been sniffing the hair spray? Been knocking back a few swigs of permanent wave solution? Need I remind you that* wrinkled *was another thing you didn't want to be when you grew up. Take a chill pill, girl.*

Cheeks flushed with new resolve, I make eye contact with my white-haired friend who thinks she's discovered the secret to simplicity. "I was born a blonde," I say to her, "and I plan to be embalmed as one."

Georgia Faye lays a smirk on me. "Haw!" She spits it out while eying the large bowl of malt balls sitting on the table in front of her. Without the slightest hint of guilt, she reaches over and pops four of the chocolates into her mouth at one time. Chewing the candy with gusto, she looks as though it could be her first taste of Godiva chocolate like they sell in gold boxes at Bloomingdale's, a store in which she will never set foot.

"You're gonna get a zit," I tell her. "A zit with wrinkles."

She cocks her head to the side and says, "Ya think?"

"I know. No matter how old you get, Georgia Faye, you never outgrow chocolate zits. Eat a Hershey Bar today and tomorrow you're talking face peel."

A smile begins to form on Georgia Faye's lipstick-less mouth as she bats her mascara-less eyelashes at me.

"Watch my lips, girlfriend. This is called low maintenance. Get it?"

"Oh, I get it all right. Now, watch *my* lips, Georgia Faye. I shall NOT go gentle into that good night. Depend on me to rage, rage against the dying of the light."

She throws up her hands. "That's it. I give up. You win."

"You give up?"

"Well, duh. I'm not about to argue with Dylan Thomas." She pauses. "Besides, to be perfectly honest, you would look like hell with a crop of white hair."

She shakes her head, pops four more malt balls into her mouth and smirks, showing off every one of her chocolate covered, unbleached teeth.

THE FAT LADY SINGS
AT LAST

"We'll Always Have Paris."—Rick to Ilisa in *Casablanca*

Much Obliged

"God is great, God is good, let us thank him for our..."

Like many of us do each day, Jack's Uncle George said grace before meals. Unlike most Southerners, however, economy of words was Uncle George's strong suit. It pleased him that people thought of him as a master of brevity. Folding his hands with a great deal of ceremony at the table, he would bow his head for a moment before commencing to bless the food by saying, "Much obliged."

It is the end of December and another twelve months have gone by. Once again, we are all preparing for the proverbial fat lady to sing. I find myself being pulled back through the past year and to all of the events that made a profound difference in my life. I had a few mishaps, but they weren't terrible. More blessings than I can count came my way and those are what I now choose to remember.

For the year about to come to a close, I am much obliged.

When Babe was diagnosed with Cancer, it shook us both to the core. Cancer wasn't supposed to happen to us! But it did, and he pulled through with the support of family and friends. The surgery was not nearly as horrific as he had feared and his last checkup could not have been better. He is Cancer free today, feels terrific, plays more golf and bridge than ever and is more loving and lovable every day.

For Babe's renewed health and vigor and for the love we share, I am much obliged.

I had another birthday and reached the age where most people retire or at least think about it. That hurt. Lord, how it hurt! But my Social Security check came through with a nice little pick-me-up that promises to be delivered to my door each and every month. I am told that we may someday run out of Social Security funds, so I am much obliged that the well has not yet run dry.

I looked in the mirror one day and asked myself who was that overweight person staring back at me. Unfortunately, she answered me and I did not like what she said. I went on a diet and fought like a Tasmanian devil to get rid of the extra pounds, and lost twenty-five of them. I'm not looking to find them again, but in case I do, you can bet I will enjoy every minute of the hunt. For shedding the twenty-five chocolate peanut butter-filled pounds, I am much obliged.

My oldest son and his wife announced that another baby boy was on the way and Thomas came into the world in December. The most beautiful baby in the world couldn't wait for Christmas, so he came early, just in time for Santa Claus. My son's new baby has given him a new lease on life and to see them together is a wonderful thing. Happiness and love are written all over his face. What mother would want any less for her child?

For the birth of my new grandson and for my own son's happiness and peace of mind, I am much obliged.

Three years ago when *Simply Southern* was published, I was delighted. I wasn't sure I would have the tenacity to follow it with another book, but I was wrong. *Simply Christmas* came out in November of the following year, and people bought it and were still buying it a year later. This past November a cookbook I co-authored with Barbara Jean Barta came out. Barbara Jean is a popular and successful restaurateur on the island, and the collaboration was a huge success. I hope the stories I wrote for the cookbook will bring laughter and good eating to everyone who buys it.

For my love of writing and for my ability to do what I love, I am truly much obliged.

The past year brought wonderful new friends into my life, and even some old acquaintances reappeared. People I have known most of my life, like Judy Hines, Janice Beane and Randolph Smith became closer to me than ever before. The Doodah Sisterhood continues to light up my life with love and laughter and more heart than I can put into words. These girlfriends of mine fill some of the blank spaces of my life with their loyalty, enthusiasm and good humor. Not only that, they actually allow me to write about them without the threat of a lawsuit.

Over the past year, three of our dearest friends left this world for a better place. The pain of losing them has been hard on both Babe and me. Wallace Prince played college football with Babe and he was truly a prince of a man. His renewed friendship over the past decade meant more to us than I can say.

Babe's best friend, Bill "Willie" Lehman, died this year. He was my friend as well as the Best Man in our wedding. Willie's sense of humor coupled with the unique way he had of phrasing sentences, telling tall tales and replaying past moments, was only one of the reasons he was so loved. Babe and Willie had been close friends for a long, long time and Babe is keenly aware of the loss of his good friend. We are both, however, much obliged for having had him in our lives for as long as we did.

Losing our close friend, Don Bogdan, has been a terrible blow. Don's laughter and good humor still resonates within the walls of our home and I believe it always will. The void left when he died is one felt by everyone who ever knew him. I am much obliged to have been one of them.

Don's death was bad news, but the good news is that his wife Joan has become more than just a friend to Babe and me. We didn't take out adoption papers on her, but we would if we could. Joan is family now and we are much obliged that she occupies such a special place in our lives.

For everyone I have mentioned, and for friends K.T., Marcia, Tudy, Lynn, Carol Fox, Maggie and Patsy, I am much obliged.

In May I brought home a box containing a tiny white kitten and Babe nearly slashed my throat. This tiny white feline immediately became the bane of his existence and the joy of mine. Sleeping and purring at my feet while I write, she deigns to talk to me if and when she feels like it, and from time to time even allows me to hold her in my arms like a little baby. For blue-eyed Sophie Sorrowful, I am much obliged.

We became grandparents to two little girls in August when Babe's daughter, Laura and her husband Chris, adopted sisters. Since Laura and Chris are both only children, Babe and I wondered how on earth they would know how to handle not one, but *two* kids. Obviously, they figured it out because they have given Brianna and Alexis a loving and safe home. In return, the girls have given them the family they always hoped to have. At this writing, Babe and I have not yet met our new granddaughters, but are looking forward to the day we can hug them tightly, look heavenward and say, "Much Obliged."

This past year, I have closely watched, perhaps with the jaundiced eye of a grandmother, the emotional and physical growth of three of my grandsons. Having named them the Grandkids from Hell several years ago, they won't allow me to change that nom de plume. But how can I put that particular label on a teenage boy who plays a Rachmaninoff Prelude on the piano with the passion of the maestro himself?

And how could I ever label Burns, the middle child, slight of body but enormous of heart, with anything other than the Grandkid from Someplace Nice. His capacity for seeing into another's soul is astonishing at such a young age. He boggles my mind with his understanding and sympathetic heart.

Parker, the boy with chocolate eyes and a chocolate appetite, loves the GFH label. He somehow morphed into a ten-year-old with so much love to give that it breaks my heart, if not some of my bones when he hugs me. He is growing up fast, much more quickly than I would like, but I so easily see the man he will be someday and that vision makes me very proud.

For the Grandkids from Hell who really are not, and for little Thomas Cooper so new to our family, I am much, much obliged.

It was a long year for me with many life lessons to learn and lots of new experiences to enjoy.

I learned to trust that God would take care of Babe, our families and me.

I discovered that I don't need to fret about whether or not the sun will come up in the morning because it's not in my job description anyhow. It's God's job.

I learned to channel my fear of the insane Iraqi terrorists into more manageable fears. Nowadays I am more likely to fret about whether I'll run out of gas or have the money to pay for it before I get to the cheap filling station at the end of the causeway.

At times during the year I was afraid I might wake up one night with a craving for chocolate that simply would not go away. My fear was not the craving, but that I would sneak into my secreted stash only to find that Babe had gotten there before me and gobbled up every piece of my clandestine chocolate.

Lord, for learning to trust that there is always enough, including chocolate, to go around and for learning how *not* to worry about every little thing, I am much obliged.

When we begin the midnight countdown this year, Babe and I will toast the new kid on the block, the year 2007, filled with hopes and dreams. We will clink glasses with some of our dearest friends and wish each other only the best for the coming year.

For all of our friends and for the possibility of hanging around for yet another day, I am much obliged.

I've got just one more thing to say before the fat lady sings…I am very much obliged for having finally finished writing this book!

ABOUT THE AUTHOR

Cappy Hall Rearick, an award winning short story writer and columnist, is the author of three previous books, *Christmas Past, Simply Southern* and *Simply Christmas.* She has recently completed writing her first novel and is presently writing, *Rocky Bottom,* another collection of short stories.

Rearick lives on St. Simons Island, Georgia with husband Bill, a Cockapoo named Tallulah Blankhead and a cat she calls Sophie Sorrowful.

978-0-595-39170-7
0-595-39170-2